Despondent Souls

Killer≠Hero Book 1

Written By:

S.M. Maldo

Despondent Souls - Killer≠Hero Series Book 1

Paperback

ISBN: 979-8-9942678-1-3

Independently Published

A special thank you to:

My gremlin, my first and still biggest fan

&

My husband, the man who pushed me to
reach for the sky.

Now...

Let me tell you a story...

1

The Beginning

20 June

Boreal Forest, Russia

The wind swept between the tall birch trees as the clouds painted shadows across the land. Amongst the rolling hills, a small village nestled comfortably on its own. It was simple yet inviting, with log homes covered in shining tin roofs. The road wound back and forth up the hillside, allowing room for everyone to live comfortably together.

Although the village was simple, it was still something to behold. The ambiance and feeling of family amongst the serenity could be felt in the air.

The locals donned simple summer dresses and jeans as they went about their day. The men chopped the lumber for the furnaces as the women took care of their homes. A few were cooking an afternoon lunch for all to enjoy, while others were cleaning laundry next to a small river towards the far side. Even the children smiled and laughed as they played at the small set of swings nestled under one of the larger trees.

Well...most of them anyway.

CRASH!

A small group of children, between the ages of 7 and 13, laughed loudly as they came around one of the houses near the outskirts. Close behind was a rather angry-looking man with a bowl on his head. Though odd, this seemed like a usual occurrence since most of the wives tried to hide their giggles, and some of the fathers looked on with a shake of their heads.

One of the young boys ran from the group and hid amongst the trees outlining the village. The older man looked around but quickly continued his chase.

The boy giggled as he watched the rest of his group vanish behind one of the houses as their pursuer followed. He wiped the sweat from his forehead with the bottom of his shirt and plopped his butt on the ground.

He smiled as he leaned against one of the trunks. He knew the other kids were going to get caught and given a stern talk, but he wasn't.

Nope.

He got away.

As he relished in his victory, he pulled a miniature toy horse from his pocket. It was simple, but anyone could tell he cherished it.

He pranced the little horse around the beams of sunlight with the occasional neigh or gallop, which broke the sounds of nature around him.

Meanwhile...

The older man stood over the other children, his finger pointed and his Russian voice echoing.

They had finally run out of breath and had to listen as they were scolded from top to bottom. As the man finished, one of the oldest boys in the group looked around. It seemed like his younger brother had been the little ninja who darted towards the woods.

After they all apologized in unison, he ran off to find his brother.

It took him no time to retrace his steps and head towards the tree line.

Though his brother knew not to go too deep into the forest alone, he wasn't sure where he'd hidden himself away. He looked behind a few trees before he let out a small sigh, followed by his brother's name.

Call after call went unanswered until the brother started to get angry.

He started to think his little brother wasn't answering on purpose.

His voice grew louder and more irritated with each call until he huffed up and crossed his arms.

He'd show him who's boss!

As he turned to leave, he misjudged his step and tripped over a tree root. He face-planted into the grass and, after lying there for a second or so, pushed himself up and looked to see which root had caught him.

He was somewhat confused at first since the tree root wasn't that tall, but his eyes slowly grew wider as he noticed something wedged in front of it.

His heart raced as he pushed himself up, tripping over his own feet as he ran towards the village. Tears gathered in his eyes as he screamed for his mom and dad.

He had to find them and fast.

For what had caused him to trip was his brother's toy horse lodged between a set of blood-stained roots.

2

Codenames: Viper and Wendigo

25 June

Brooklyn, New York

The sun set slowly against the horizon, casting its radiant reds and golds across the mountainous skyscrapers. Though the city buzzed with life, an odd peace seemed to pervade the crowds; a normality often found in the city of dreams.

However, an unbridled chaos flourished within.

Never sleeping.

As the daylight baked the sidewalks, the businessmen and office workers rotted in their home away from home. They sat behind their cubicle prisons and high-rise caves, justifying their actions in the name of love for their broken family.

But, after the sun vanished beyond the horizon and the abundance of streetlights and signs hid the moon, another world appeared.

Business dealings and bartering crowded the small alleyways. The muffled screams and cries of desire seeped from the hotel windows. Countless clubs and bars bustled as alcohol drowned once proud men into fools.

The skyscrapers towered above the streets with specks of light sporadically coloring their sides; some so high they were mistaken for stars. The cause was mostly the bottom feeders of the cut-throat corporate world. The ones made to suffer into the wee hours of the morning doing work that wasn't even theirs.

Having said that, there was one star that didn't fall in with the rest.

Its subtle light graced the far reaches of the night sky. Inside the studio-size office sat a very handsome man. The soft white from the lights buried in the ceiling illuminated his rather masculine features. Behind him was a wall-length window that framed the city like a gorgeous painting.

He reclined back in his seat as a small sigh escaped his full and luscious lips. His hand raked through his short black hair before he reached into the pocket of his rather expensive gray suit and removed a cigar.

As he placed it in his mouth, he leaned forward and grabbed the cutter from a small dish on the corner of his large but immaculately clean desk. A subtle but noticeable placard rested beside it:

Killian Blackwell

CEO

It was obvious to anyone that he was a man not to be trifled with.

His physique also helped his powerful aura, though.

The muscles in his arms rippled through his suit as he leaned back after he grabbed the cutter. They flexed again as he clipped the tip and threw it away. One could say his suit was a size too small, but that wasn't the case.

He was just that well-defined.

He then reached into his chest pocket to remove a Zippo lighter. After he pulled it out, he paused and stared at the small engraving on its side. His thumb softly rubbed against it. There were no initials or names, but just a date:

January 19th.

A soft half-smile eased onto his face as he popped it open and puffed in to light the cigar. As the smoke surrounded his sharply defined features, he gently returned the lighter back to his coat. He turned the chair slowly and took in the sea of lights from his window.

He took a slight drag and just as he began to relax...

KNOCK! KNOCK!

A second passed.

He released a small sigh as he turned back, the smoke wrapping around him.

"What now?" He muttered with a slightly annoyed expression.

"Enter."

The large double doors opened slowly as a rather large and muscular man made his way in. His long black hair was parted to one side and held loosely by a ribbon as his green eyes stood out against his somewhat tanned skin.

He was model material for sure.

Or Pro-Wrestling.

Either would've suited him.

After a few long strides, he stopped and stood at attention before Killian. The smoke from the cigar danced across the desk and enveloped his body slowly.

"You have a phone call from your father, Mr. Blackwell," he stated as he removed a small cellphone from his inside pocket and placed it on the desk. The screen showed the call already in progress with the speaker on mute.

Killian took another draw as he took the phone.

"Thank you, Stephen. You can leave now," he responded in a rather lax tone as he tapped the ashes from the tip and rested the cigar in the small bowl from earlier.

Stephen bowed his head and excused himself.

However, before he could make it out of the office,

"Stephen," Killian stated.

Stephen stopped in his tracks and turned around. "Yes, Mr. Blackwell."

"I have a feeling I'll be needing to take a leave of absence after this phone call. Be sure to update all my meetings and such as needed," he said as he stood and turned towards the window, the ambiance of city lights outlining his figure.

"Right away, Sir," He responded, then excused himself. He grabbed the double doors and closed them, the echo resounding around the office.

Killian then unmuted the phone and answered with, "Hello, Boss."

The man on the other side laughed out loud as he responded, "Boss? Is that any way to greet your father, Killian? You make me sound like I'm old enough to kick the bucket already."

He couldn't hold it back any longer.

His intimidating, cold expression melted into one of warmth and comfort as a smile broke through. "I couldn't help it. It's been a while since I last heard from you. I think you were in…Asia the last time we spoke."

"I think you're right!" the man confirmed in laughter. "I didn't realize it had been that long." There was a slight pause. "It's good to hear your voice again, son."

Killian's smile grew as he turned back towards his desk and picked up the still-lit cigar. "Same to you, old man," he said as he took a draw. "So what do I owe the pleasure?"

"Straight to the point! I see I raised you right," he responded. "Well, as you might have guessed, I'm calling you for business." Although his tone was more serious, it was still filled with love.

"And what business requires you to call me yourself?"

"It's concerning the route in Russia."

Killian's expression hardened.

"What about the route in Russia?"

"It seems someone or *something* is attacking the villagers we have at our checkpoint. And it's not just our checkpoint. Seems some of our partners have also had a few of their own go missing."

There was a short silence before Killian asked, "*Which* partners?" His attitude made it clear that he suspected who it was but sincerely hoped he was wrong.

His father let out a sigh as he said, "It's who you think it is."

"Damnit," Killian muttered as he sat back down. "So, will one of their own be joining me again? Last time it ended with the coward dying at the hands of some mercenaries, and I don't want to have to deal with the paperwork for something like that again."

Laughter echoed, followed by a moment for his father to catch his breath. "I'm glad to know the organization will be in good hands when I retire. You're the perfect man to take over my position."

Smoke melted into the air as Killian leaned back. "You're not dead yet old man. I'm just doing all the hard work, but the title is still yours." A smile broke through once more. "I'll take the title in due time."

A snicker was heard as his father regained his composure. "Fair enough, but I will need you to do some grunt work for this one. I don't trust anyone as much as you. Besides, the villagers there know you well."

"I'll take care of the issue."

He held the phone to his head with his shoulder and rested the cigar in the bowl before he started typing away on the double-monitor computer in front of him. "So, who *is* going to be my partner for the mission?"

There was a slight pause.

A slight pause that made Killian very uncomfortable and worried.

"Father?" He asked with annoyed concern. "Who is my partner?"

The older man sighed. "Your partner is going to be Wendigo."

The utter look of surprise Killian wore quickly melted into disdain. "What do you mean, my partner is going to be Wendigo?"

By that time, he had grabbed the phone and needed to restrain his desire to throw it at the window.

"You mean *the* Wendigo? The one who got in the way of my deal with the Japanese because he was after their leader? The one who got in my way in Germany because the man he was after just so happened to be the spy I had put there?" THAT Wendigo?"

"Yes," his father stated bluntly. "And you will work alongside him to solve this issue without fail. Do I make myself clear?" The once-relaxed, easy tone was replaced with authority and demand.

Killian's grip and jaw tightened as he restrained himself. "Yes, Sir. I will take care of it." His tone was low and emotionless.

"Good," the other man responded with a fatherly tone. "Now that the business is out of the way, I am going to continue my partial retirement and will be in touch. Stay safe, son."

"Wai..."

BEEP BEEP BEEP

"You old son of a bitch," Killian muttered as he set the phone down. He leaned forward and rested his hands on the desk as a deep sigh escaped. "Out of everyone," he paused as he looked over to his computer. On the screen was the file his father had sent, which included information about his soon-to-be partner. "Why did it have to be him?"

Meanwhile,

In Chicago, IL

As if a mirror image of Brooklyn, the nightlife raged on down the streets of Chicago.

Music blared from the clubs lining the cubed streets, and apart from the occasional drunk passed out against the walls, everyone seemed to be having a grand time.

BAM!

Well...*almost* everyone.

The sound from the large metal door hitting the brick wall echoed down the long alleyway behind one such club as a very handsome man came outside.

His short, messy black hair accentuated his fair complexion and complemented his bright Egyptian blue eyes. The tight black t-shirt and relaxed-fit jeans he wore hugged his curves as if he were a model. His defined arms were not large, but it was obvious he worked out. The definition of his chest was also a dead giveaway.

Although his appearance was handsome to say the least, his expression was a stark contrast. It was apparent he was really, *really* pissed about something as he held a small flip phone firmly against his defined jawline.

"Whadya mean I have to team up with the Viper?!" His voice was deep, and one could tell there was a hint of Northern in there.

"It's exactly like I said," responded an older man's voice through the phone. "You will be teaming up with the Viper to resolve a 'mutual' issue."

"And what 'mutual issue' would that be?! HM?!"

It was obvious his anger and frustration were growing as he paced back and forth down the alley.

"There is NO reason the CIA should have *anything* to do with the Syndicate! Considering one upholds rules and regulations while the other does nothing but BREAK said rules and regulations."

He wasn't wrong.

There was hardly anyone in the world who hadn't heard of the Syndicate.

They were the most prominent crime organization by far, with headquarters located in Russia, South Korea, Brazil, Australia, Greenland, and the US. The majority of underground activity involving money, drugs, weapons, slavery, and warfare was handled by one of the six Monarchs, with one located in each country.

The older man let out an aggravated sigh as he responded.

"Last I checked, Agent Hawke Everhart, you are an operative of the Special Activities Division, and when I give you an order, you acknowledge and get it done. Why is this time any different?"

"Why is….," Hawke stumbled over his words for a second as he took in a deep breath. Between clenched teeth, he responded with, "I understand my role as an operative, but what I don't understand is why I'm having to partner with a man who has been nothing but a thorn in our ass for the last 5 years!" He rubbed his hand down his face as he stopped pacing and leaned against the far wall away from the small lights above the back entrance.

Small clicking noises echoed over the phone as the older man took in and let out a deep breath from lighting his cigarette.

"The reason you are getting involved is because *I* need *you* to make sure the mission is a success," he stated. "This mission is of the utmost importance."

Hawke's anger swelled.

"And if it's THAT important, I need ta know all the details!"

After a brief pause and an irritated sigh, the older man responded. "This mission is off the books. There's a chance there is a larger force at work that undermines both the CIA and the Syndicate. Our sides have decided that a cease-fire to topple a common enemy is the best course of action."

Hawke's mood did not improve after hearing that.

In fact...

It got worse.

"I don't give a damn if there's a common enemy between the CIA and the Syndicate. I don't give a damn if the end of the world is coming. I WILL NOT partner with that piece of shit!" With each word, his voice rose and his anger swelled.

The older man's attitude changed drastically as a loud slam reverberated over the phone as his fist hit the desk.

"And I don't give a damn if you like this mission or not! You either complete this mission and get the job done, or you will be demoted and do paperwork at the front desk for the rest of your life!" He retorted.

Hawke clenched his fist so hard a trickle of blood dripped from his finger.

"Un-der-stood, Sir," he enunciated each syllable slowly. "Just know this will be the last mission I ever do for you."

The older man thundered with laughter. "We'll see about that, Agent Everhart."

Instantly, Hawke realized he wouldn't be allowed to resign even if he wanted to.

"You leave for Russia in 48 hours. I will send you the details shortly, which will include the location for take-off," his boss stated. "Safe travels."

BEEP. BEEP. BEEP.

Hawke slowly took the phone from his face and folded it shut with one hand.

The whole situation was still sinking in, but he didn't have time to think.

With slow, methodical strides, he made his way down the alley towards the cheap motel he was staying in and scratched the back of his head.

"This is gonna suck so fucking much," he mumbled.

And oh, how right he would be.

3

Time for Take Off

27 June

A Private Airport

Killian leaned against the opening of the hangar. His small but private landing strip was nestled on Huckleberry Island outside of New York. The peace and tranquility of the forest were one of the main reasons Killian had chosen this area as his base years ago. That, and it was close enough to everything for convenience but far enough away to quell suspicion when a random airplane took off out of nowhere.

The hustle of workers readying the plane for take-off mixed with the small sounds of nature. Technicians and mechanics worked like a well-oiled machine.

"We'll be ready to head out in about twenty minutes, boss."

Killian turned to his lead mechanic, who was covered in grease and oil. The man stood eye to eye with him, figuratively and literally. His dirty blonde dreads, light brown eyes, and rather formidable figure complemented his worn-out overalls and military boots.

"Thank you, David," he responded as he turned around. "How's the family been? I bet the baby is getting bigger every day." He rested his hands in his pockets, which was an odd gesture for him. It showed how comfortable he felt around them.

Which was a stark contrast to his normal "on-guard" stature.

Of course, when one was raised in the underworld, trust wasn't something easily given.

"Getting meaner too," David joked as he wiped his hands on a nearby shop towel. "I can already tell he's going to be just like his dad."

"God, help us all then," Killian jokingly responded.

David bellowed in laughter before he said, "I'll let ya know once I finish everything up." As he spoke, he bowed his head and made his way over to one of the other workers who was checking the engine intake.

As he watched them, Killian couldn't help but let a small smirk escape. Everyone there was magnificent in their field but wouldn't have known their own potential if it hadn't been for him. All of them were from less-than-ideal backgrounds or situations.

In normal society, they were shunned and ridiculed.

That was the main reason Killian had invested the necessary money and time to turn them into his own personal and private force.

He knew what it was like to be looked down on.

He knew what it was like to have entitled spigots spit on you when all you asked for was a drink of water.

It was something he wouldn't wish on *almost* anyone.

As he reminisced quietly, he reached inside his suit and pulled out one of his cigars, quickly followed by his lighter. As he released his first billow of smoke, it circled around and slowly vanished above him.

And just as he finished putting his lighter back, Killian felt something hit the back of his legs.

THUD!

He slowly turned to see a young boy sitting on the ground with tears gathering in his eyes and a couple of tools spread around. Sporting a gray t-shirt and cargo pants, he recognized him as one of David's younger sons.

With a smile, he removed the cigar from his mouth and knelt to the boy's level.

"I'm so sorry, Sir!" The young boy frantically apologized as he reached around and picked up the collection of tools he'd been carrying. "I wasn't looking where I was going and,"

Killian placed his free hand on top of the boy's as he reached for a socket wrench. The boy stopped and looked up, tears trying so hard to break through his attempt to hold them back.

"What's your name?" Killian asked in a soft tone.

"Ale-Alexander, Sir," he stuttered as his cheeks started to flush from embarrassment.

"Alexander," Killian said as he picked up the wrench and held it out for him. "That's a strong name.

How about you just be a bit more careful next time, ok?"

"Y-Yes, Sir!" Alexander stated rather loudly as he took the wrench. He stood up with all the tools in hand and bowed before darting towards David, who was at the end of the plane.

As he stood back up, Killian took a small draw from his cigar. He let out a sigh as he took a moment to look at his watch. It was already after five in the afternoon.

His mood shifted.

And not for the better.

"The one time I wait for you to pop up, you run late," he mumbled as the smoke escaped his lips.

VROOM!

A loud roaring noise came from the other side of the hangar.

Killian cocked his brow as he looked around the corner. When he saw what made the noise, he let out the smoke with an irritated sigh.

It was Hawke driving a 1970 Plymouth Barracuda. The 426 modified Hemi roared as he came up the runway, and, in what seemed like seconds, stopped in front of Killian. Didn't take him long to grab his bag from the passenger seat and exit his chariot, either. As he stood there, dressed in a tight black tank and military pants with boots to match, he gave Killian a once-over.

"Nice of you to finally join us," Killian mocked as he put out his cigar against the hangar wall. "I was wondering if I was going to have to call your boss and see if you had died before the mission even started."

Hawke's jaw ticked as he adjusted the bag over his shoulder. "Well, I'm sorry that it took me a while to find the *hidden* airstrip on an island that I've never been to," he said as he leaned in, their faces almost touching. "Sorry, I kept you waiting."

The sheer level of sarcasm in his apology could have made a mime gasp.

Killian was not surprised by his less-than-professional attitude.

"It's alright. I didn't expect much from a CIA lap dog in the first place," Killian responded before he turned and moved inside the hangar. "It is rather sad, though. That you arrived in such a nice car instead of a body bag."

Hawke scoffed at the remark as he followed behind. Although this was enemy territory, he couldn't help but be impressed. The level of dedication the workers had was evident in how they worked and carried themselves.

"You can go ahead and board," Killian stated as he stood beside the small stairs that led inside. "I have a few more items to check on before we take off." Before Hawke could respond, he walked away.

"It seems manners are in short supply," Hawke grumbled under his breath as he made his way up the stairs and boarded the jet.

Inside, it sported a gray carpet floor with foreign designs sewn in with black thread. A couch sat against the starboard side, and four very comfortable seats rested closer to the cockpit, two on each side with their fronts facing one another.

Before he moved past in the entrance, a young lady, possibly in her mid-twenties, came up to him from the tail end and smiled. With a polite bow of her head, she asked, "May I take your bag, Sir?" Her Middle Eastern accent was slight but suited her well.

"Sure. Thank you," he casually responded as he brought the bag around and handed it to her. The bag was on the larger side, so he said, "I can help you with that if – "

"No need, Sir. Now, if you would care to take your seat, we will be taking off shortly," she interrupted as she grabbed the bag from his hands.

Hawke was unable to respond before she excused herself to put the bag away.

He had to admit, though, she was strong *and* beautiful.

In fact, he couldn't help but watch as she walked away. Although she appeared small and frail, the strength it took to carry his bag alongside the definition in her body quickly quelled those assumptions. Her long, braided black hair swayed in tune with her hips and thighs as she walked. The small black dress she wore covered her from mid-thigh to barely above her chest. The supple bounce her D cups gave as she reached up towards the luggage bin above her station was almost too much to handle.

He bit the corner of his lip as he shook his head.

"Damn," he mumbled under his breath as he made his way to the four seats up front.

As he sat, he caught movement from the corner of his eye and turned around.

When he did, he noticed a small boy helping an older man check the landing gear. The boy looked like he was having the time of his life as he handed over one tool after another. The man smiled as he ruffled the boy's hair, which made the little guy laugh.

In fact, Hawke couldn't help but crack a smile.

Unfortunately, it also brought up some unsavory memories.

Images of his father raced through his mind, followed quickly by anger and resentment. He shook his head to banish the feelings and images as he noticed Killian making his way over.

They struck up a conversation, and even the boy seemed comfortable around him. There was something odd about the conversation, though.

The way Killian held himself was different from what Hawke had imagined.

Based on the information he was given in the file, he had imagined Killian as a tyrant. A man who stepped on those beneath him and instilled fear in everyone he came in contact with.

The man outside the plane was far from that.

If he'd not known what Killian was capable of, he would've thought he was just a regular guy chatting it up with an old friend.

But he definitely knew better.

Not just from the intel he read through, but from moments he'd witnessed himself. The man was a cold-blooded killer when it was needed.

He watched as Killian excused himself. When he did, the man and the young boy bowed with their right arms across their chests in respect and subservience.

What exactly have you done to deserve this level of respect, Blackwell?

He barely finished the thought before Killian boarded, and the stewardess greeted him with a smile. Killian smiled back and gently patted her on the top of her head with his free hand. The action was rather odd for someone as dark and foreboding as Killian Blackwell, but the young lady seemed elated by the action as she turned and made her way to hang up the coat he had removed upon entering.

Hawke couldn't help but be minutely impressed by Killian's build as he walked towards the seats. In all the photos he'd seen and all the times he'd caught a glimpse himself he always had a suit on.

He had to give the guy credit.

Killian had the body to back up his pride and smug demeanor.

"Are you done staring?" Killian questioned as he sat down across from him. "Or would you like to snap a picture to enjoy later?"

As he then re-lit the cigar from earlier and smoke swirled around him, Hawke glared.

"I think I'm good. I have a feeling I'm gonna get enough of you to last a lifetime," he scoffed as he relaxed back in his seat.

Killian couldn't help but snicker.

"You've got some balls, I'll give you that," he said as he relaxed in his seat. "Most people wouldn't dare to talk to me in such a way."

Hawke locked eyes with him as he leaned forward and rested his arms on his knees. "Well, you definitely don't have to worry about me filtering what I say to you." The tone of his voice and the smirk he wore left no doubt about how cynical he was being.

Killian also adjusted his position and leaned in close, their faces now only inches apart. "Same goes for you, bird boy."

Hawke's eye twitched at the insult. Although Killian couldn't have known, it was a nickname he had through school and one he absolutely hated.

Killian picked up on his reaction, and his smirk grew.

"Guess I hit a nerve, huh?"

Hawke's eyes filled with rage.

"Would either of you gentlemen care for a drink before we take off?"

The soft, feminine voice calmed him down as he looked over and saw the stewardess standing beside them. Her face made it obvious their verbal altercation had no effect whatsoever, but Hawke couldn't help but let out an aggravated sigh.

"I will take a Jack and Coke," he stated as he receded first and leaned back again.

As he did so, Killian followed suit but was sure to make it obvious he won this round by keeping his grin.

"I will take my usual dear," Killian answered, but kept his eyes focused on Hawke.

"Coming right up," the stewardess responded as she bowed softly and excused herself.

Hawke watched as she walked away and couldn't help but have a naughty passing thought run through his mind. That is, until he noticed something he'd missed earlier. His emotions jumped from desire to confusion, then anger.

Which was then quickly turned towards Killian.

"Do you normally treat all your employees with such care?" He questioned with an obvious tick to his words.

Killian cocked his brow in confusion.

He had no idea what he was talking about.

As he looked over, however, he saw what sparked the question.

The slits in the back of her dress revealed scars littered across her back. They ranged in size from small to large, deep to shallow. There was no rhyme or reason to their placement.

He placed his cigar between his lips and inhaled. The smoke wrapped around his face, but enveloped Hawke as he released his breath in full force.

"You know," Killian's tone was subtle, but the irritation he felt was evident. "Maybe you shouldn't jump to conclusions so quickly."

Hawke was unfazed.

"Why would I have any reason to believe otherwise?" Hawke smarted off.

Killian's jaw ticked as he tapped his cigar in the small ashtray to the side of his seat. He had no reason to give Hawke any information about his employees, but the sheer audacity Hawke had to make outlandish assumptions rattled him for some reason.

"She got those scars from her previous employer," he began. "She was a prostitute I found in an alleyway during one of my business trips. Her last client showed his love in a very forceful way."

The surprised and disgusted look on Hawke's face eased his irritation a bit.

"I decided to buy her. After nursing her back to health and finding out which brothel she belonged to, the Mother and I had a heart-to-heart, and she became mine."

As he finished, the young stewardess returned. She politely set Hawke's drink to his right, followed by

Killian's drink. He used his free arm to pull her close to him and momentarily rest his head on his stomach.

Once again, never breaking eye contact with Hawke.

"Aura makes my flights much more enjoyable," he slowly enunciated as his hand adjusted to rest on her butt.

Aura smiled down at Killian as she blushed ever so slightly.

It was obnoxiously obvious what they were talking about.

With a look of defeat buried beneath his scowl, he picked up his drink and took his first sip as he leaned back.

"I bet she does," he stated as he rested his hand and twirled the ice in his glass. "I apologize for the misunderstanding."

A deaf mime could tell his apology was far from sincere, but Killian didn't care. Just hearing it was enough for him.

"Apology accepted," he responded as he released his grip on Aura, who took this chance to excuse herself.

Killian watched as she sauntered away.

"I don't get you, Blackwell," Hawke stated abruptly.

The look of surprise on Killian's face made it clear he hadn't expected Hawke's random remark.

"According to every bit of information I could gather on you, you're a heartless, cynical, bloodthirsty demon in human skin who has no regard for any life other than your own, but," he paused as he glanced down to his glass, "your underlings revere you as a saint."

Killian paused as he glanced to the side, catching a small glimpse of Aura cleaning up her station.

"I could say the same about you, Mr. Everhart," Killian commented, looking back and tilting his glass so Hawke's face was visible through the liquid. "You are the top undercover agent in the CIA, have more awards for your excellence than any other operative, and can have your pick of any woman you want, but," he also took a moment to pause as he brought his glass down and took a drink.

"No matter how thoroughly I dug or how many avenues I explored, I couldn't find out anything about you before your enlistment at the age of 18. It's like your whole life prior never happened. As if you manifested from thin air."

"Guess that's something we have in common then," Hawke stated as he stopped twirling his glass and locked eyes with him. "Which makes the reason

I'm on this mission with you that much more infuriating."

RUMBLE!

The jet jerked slightly.

They were leaving the hangar.

Killian couldn't help but agree with Hawke. "I don't like this arrangement any more than you do, so I suggest we do everything we can to solve the issue quickly."

"That's the first time I think we can agree on something," Hawke responded.

After the jet took off and leveled out, they decided to exchange information. Each of them pulled out a folder with notes and print-offs to make it easier to access.

Hours flew by until Hawke set down the documents and stretched his arms high.

Killian followed suit and realized it was time to get some rest. He hadn't rested well the past few days and needed to be in top shape when they arrived.

"I think I'm going to call it a night," he stated as he stood up. "I suggest you do the same since we still have some time before we arrive," his tone more of a you-better-do-it than I-suggest-you-do-it.

"Thanks. I'll be sure to store up some beauty sleep," Hawke mumbled under his breath as he gathered the papers and set them beside him in the other seat. He looked over as Killian made his way past Aura to what he assumed was the sleeping quarters.

After he vanished behind the drapes covering the entrance, Aura made her way towards him.

"Do you need anything else, Mr. Everhart? We have some refreshments as well as blankets," she offered with a heartfelt smile.

There was a moment of silence as he looked into her auburn brown eyes. "What do you see in him?" He asked bluntly.

Aura looked somewhat surprised by the question but quickly answered with, "Mr. Blackwell saved me."

"Yeah. I heard a little about that, but why do ya look so happy around him? I mean, all he did was buy you. Ya just went from one servitude to another."

She shook her head.

"No. I owe my life to him," she responded with her hand fisted over her heart. "Mr. Blackwell saved me from my situation, but he's also given me everything I need. He has given me a job, sent me to school, and," she paused before she looked into his eyes, "he gave me a home."

The pure and utter sincerity in her love for him was almost too much for Hawke to handle.

Given her response, he decided to let the question go.

"Gotcha," he said as he leaned back and rested his legs in Killian's former seat. "I think I'm fine for now. If I need anything, I'll let you know, though."

Aura smiled as she excused herself and went back to her seat.

"Home, huh?" He muttered under his breath as he leaned his seat back and stared out the small window across from him. The stars and moon looked like a painting with how perfect and unbothered they were. "I wonder what that feels like."

The concept of home had always been something he couldn't quite understand. Although he had a place to live, he didn't think of it as home.

His small one-bedroom apartment was just the place where he slept and stored his things. He wasn't there most of the time anyway. He'd long since resolved himself to live as he would die:

Alone and unremembered.

"Whatever. Doesn't matter anyway," he stated under his breath. A hint of sadness highlighted his eyes before they shut. "Might as well get some sleep before we arrive. I have a feeling...this is...going to...be," he mumbled as the exhaustion from the last few days finally caught up with him.

A few hours later...

As Killian lay in his bed, he couldn't help but look at the ceiling with a sigh. With nothing to hide his devilish figure except his solid black boxers, one could truly take in his glory. The definition of his muscles and the depth of his hips accentuated his figure as the muscles in his arms flexed when he pushed himself up to sit on the edge of the bed.

Though his physique was pulled straight out of Chippendale's magazine, it was not without its imperfections.

Scars riddled his back and chest.

The slashes crisscrossed and melted into one another. It was hard to tell when one stopped and one started.

Some were deep while others were shallow.

There were even a few gunshot wounds dotted in the most random of places.

It was hard to believe someone could live through all that carnage.

He pushed his bangs from his face as he looked out the small window to his left, admiring the same almost cosmic view of the stars and moon.

"I guess I woke up too soon," he said softly as he peered at the small clock to the side of the bed. "We still have a bit before we arrive."

As thoughts raced through his mind, he couldn't help but have a bad feeling about the whole situation.

There was something off, but he couldn't put his finger on it.

"I hope, for once, my intuition is wrong," he mumbled as he shook his head with a sigh.

"I guess we'll find out soon."

4

Arrival

28 June

A Private Air Strip in Russia

Sunlight beamed through the small windows as Hawke shuffled in his seat. He peeked his eye open but closed it instantly when he saw the sunlight outside.

Well fuck. It wasn't a nightmare after all.

A sigh escaped as he rubbed his eyes and stretched out his arms with a groan. He sat up and, after he gave his eyes a moment to adjust, he could see people and vehicles moving outside on the airstrip.

"Mr. Everhart," a familiar soft voice chimed in from the side.

He looked over to see Aura wearing a smile and holding a small glass of water.

"Mr. Blackwell left a moment ago and asked me to wake you, but it seems that wasn't necessary," she stated as she extended the glass.

Hawke groaned under his breath as he took the water. He gulped it down in one go and handed it back. As he did, he noticed his bag sat on the seat across from him. "Did you bring my bag over?" he asked.

"No," she stated as she took the cup. "Mr. Blackwell brought it over as he grabbed his own belongings."

"Hmph," was all Hawke mustered. Who would've thought that the asshole could be nice once in a while? "Well, thank you for the water, but I probably shouldn't keep his *lordship* waiting." His overly sarcastic tone to the word lordship was comical.

Aura nodded with a smile as she turned to make her way to the cockpit. Before she made it too far, though, she looked back and said, "Even though you don't like Mr. Blackwell, I think you should give him a chance. He really is a wonderful man once you get to know him."

"Thanks. I'll keep it in mind even if it's not true."

She kept her professional expression, but Hawke could tell she truly believed what she said as she turned and disappeared behind the cockpit curtain.

A wonderful man, my ass.

Hawke let out an irritated sigh as he stood and lifted the bag over his shoulder.

Must be brainwashing at its finest.

As he moved past his seat and looked back slightly, he noticed a small photo about to fall from the side pocket of his bag. He paused, then grabbed the picture.

The photo was of a small boy, probably 10 to 12 years old, with a woman crouched beside him. They both wore smiles from ear to ear, and it looked like water had been involved in whatever chaos they had made, as they were both soaked to the bone.

As he stared, a smile crept on his lips.

"Let's get this over with, Mom," he mumbled as he placed it back in the pocket and made sure to zip it closed. He then made his way down the small stairs and admired the organized chaos of the airport around him. Seemed like this airport was used by more than just Killian's private jet. A cargo plane was being offloaded across the strip with dozens of people walking in and out of it.

"Guess this is one of their drop-off spots," Hawke muttered to himself. Now he wished he had stayed up and seen where they landed. It would have been a great opportunity to bust them.

"Seems like you're planning something," a rather annoyed voice said behind him.

A scoff was let out as Hawke responded, "can't help but be in work mode when I see illegal activities going on in front of me." Once turned around, his eyes widened in surprise at Killian's change in clothes.

He stood in a tight black t-shirt that accentuated every nook and cranny of his well-defined body. The cargo shorts he wore relaxed on his hips, and his usually covered toned legs fit well in them. His sneakers looked worn but fit the outfit well.

Killian smirked as he took a few steps forward and leaned in rather uncomfortably close as he said, "What's wrong? Cat got your tongue?"

Hawke stood his ground and kept his eyes forward. "No," he stated. "I'm just not used to 'nature lover' Killian. I've only seen the 'evil businessman' persona."

Killian couldn't help himself and responded with, "Oh, I see." His breath lingered on Hawke's ear. "Do you think I'm *that* attractive?"

Hawke held his ground as his hair stood on end and a shiver ran down his spine. It was like a viper hissing in his ear. "You're not bad, but," he turned his head just so their eyes would meet. "I'm definitely the hotter one."

With a small humph and a smirk, Killian backed away and grabbed his bag from the ground. "That's a matter of opinion," he said as he lifted it over his shoulder, then made his way to the off-road, no-door Jeep parked a few feet away. "Let's get going before I give in to my desire to punch you in that pretty boy face of yours."

"Well, at least you can admit I'm pretty," Hawke taunted as he followed suit and went to the passenger side. They both tossed their bags in the back and took their respective spots as driver and passenger.

As Killian started the Jeep, he looked over. Although the guy had a mouth on him, the rest actually had some backing to it. His muscles flexed as he crossed his arms after he put on the sunglasses he'd grabbed from the top of the dashboard. Strength was definitely his maxed-out stat.

That's not surprising.

Killian thought to himself as he put on his own pair of glasses. He pulled out of the hangar, and they were on their way down a long dirt road riddled with trees and brush.

"We have about an hour before we get to the village," Killian yelled over the sound of the Jeep and air rushing around them.

"Perfect," Hawke responded as he reached down and leaned his seat back a small bit. "Wake me when we get there." And with that, he closed his eyes, crossed his arms, and fell asleep.

Killian focused on the road, but internally, he couldn't help but laugh.

He is either really stupid or really confident.

"Guess we'll see which one later," he softly said under his breath as they continued onwards.

One hour later...

After what felt like forever, Killian saw the village as they cleared a small hill.

"We're here," he yelled.

Hawke stretched out his arms and groaned before he lifted the seat and took in the surroundings. Lush forests surrounded them as the village grew closer and closer. He had to admit: the view was beautiful.

As they broke through the edge of the city, the villagers continued with their business as usual. That is, until they realized who was driving the Jeep.

"The boss is here!" One of the teenage boys yelled in English as he put down the wheelbarrow he'd been pushing.

Hawke was a bit confused and made no effort to hide it.

Since when do civilians in a Russian village speak English with no accent?

As they came to a stop in what was considered the 'parking area' outside the main stretch of the village, Killian glanced over and could see the confusion written all over his face. "Just because we're in Russia doesn't mean everyone in the village is Russian," he stated as he turned off the Jeep.

"Naw, shit, Sherlock. I gathered that, thanks," Hawke retorted as villager after villager came from all directions to meet up with them.

Killian stepped down from his seat and was instantly surrounded by some attractive women. They were talking so fast Hawke couldn't make out what they were saying, but it was evident that some were speaking English while others were speaking Russian.

What the fuck is up with this place?

Hawke grunted as he stepped down himself with a rather unamused look on his face.

"Why the long face, Hawke?" Killian asked as he looked over. "Jealous that the ladies aren't flocking to you?" His sarcastic tone irritated Hawke even more.

"Mr. Blackwell."

One of the ladies who stood in front brought his attention back.

"The elder wished to speak with you as soon as you arrived," she stated.

"Of course he does," Killian sighed as he spoke. "Well, I can't keep the old geezer waiting. He might kick the bucket before I make it over there." His comment made a few of the ladies laugh. Without looking back, he stated, "I'll be back in a bit. Be sure to play nice with the villagers."

Hawke's jaw ticked as he turned to remark but was quickly shut down by what he saw. The young ladies who had been fawning over him, as well as the other villagers in his path, stepped to the side and bowed their heads as he passed. It was like an old 'King in ancient time' 90s movie.

He couldn't stop himself from mouthing *What the hell* as he turned back around. However, he was greeted by some new guests when he did.

"Hey, Mister!"

Hawke jerked slightly as the small voice surprised him. What was even more surprising was the fact that he'd been surrounded...

By children.

There were at least eight boys and girls varying in age, all staring up at him.

"Mister?" He asked in confusion. "I'm not *that* old. Just call me Hawke."

"Ok, Uncle Hawke," another one of the boys stated.

Before Hawke could argue against his new title, the kids bamboozled him with questions followed by tugs on his shirt and pants. Their ages seemed to range from toddler to young adult, but that didn't matter to Hawke since he couldn't make out anything they were saying. Their voices melted together into one ear-bleeding bonanza.

"Children!" A young lady yelled as she walked up.

The kids flinched as they slowly turned in unison.

"He is a guest," she stated as she pushed her way through and stopped beside Hawke. "And what do we do for guests?" Her pale complexion and chocolate brown eyes stood out instantly. She appeared to be in her early twenties. Her long, floral summer dress gently wrapped around her petite figure. She was beautiful.

A few seconds passed before the kids' faces lit back up and they all yelled, "We cook!"

"That's right," she confirmed with a sing-song tone. "So why don't you kids go help the others get ready for the feast we're going to have tonight?"

Before Hawke could do anything else, the kids scattered in all directions. It was like a magic trick with how fast they all vanished. Well, all except one little toddler-aged girl who was still latched onto the bottom of his pants.

He looked down and couldn't help but smile as she looked back up with her thumb in her mouth. Her long brown hair rested messily, and her light blue eyes radiated innocence. She then released his pants and the thumb from her mouth, but only long enough to reach up high and groan a bit.

She wanted to be picked up.

"Now, Elisa," the young lady said as she moved a little closer and crouched down. "You know our guest needs to take his things to the house before we get ready for supper, right? And he can't do that if he's carrying you too." Her long, braided, brown hair fell from her shoulder as she tilted her head to the side with a smile.

Elisa looked over to her for a moment. A small pause made it seem like she understood, but she decided to ignore the suggestion altogether. She turned back towards Hawke but was armed with a small tear in her eye when she did.

Hawke sighed in defeat.

"Don't worry about it," he said as he reached into the back of the Jeep for his bag, quickly latched it across his chest, then picked up Elisa. "I don't mind."

It was a rather odd sight-seeing a hardened CIA agent with his gear bag on and a toddler nestled in his arms.

The young lady stood back up and smiled. "Thanks. She can be a little spoiled sometimes." She dusted herself off, then bowed her head politely. "My name is Clarice."

Hawke smiled and responded, "Mine is Hawke."

"Well, Hawke," she stated as she stood beside him. "How about I show you to the house you'll be staying in while you're here?"

"Thank you. That would be nice." His tone was soft; a stark contrast from the snarky-pissed-off attitude he had when he boarded the plane.

Hawke and Clarice made their way back down the dirt road as Elisa rested her body against Hawke's arm and rested her head against his chest as she resumed her thumb-sucking. They were about halfway through town before Hawke had decided to try his luck and see if he could get any information about his temporary partner.

"Do ya mind if I ask ya a question?"

"Of course not." Her instant response caught Hawke off guard. Usually, people hesitated when one started a conversation off like that.

"Why do you," he paused as he tried to get his wording right. "Why does the village?" He just couldn't say it without sounding like a complete jerk.

A small giggle escaped her lips before she said, "Why do we seem to enjoy working under Mr. Blackwell? That's what you were trying to ask, right?"

Hawke sighed as he moved a small piece of hair from Elisa's cheek. "Yeah," he responded, but didn't look back over.

Clarice smiled. "I can't tell you too much, but," she paused as she stopped at the doorway to the house the two men would be staying in. "What I can tell you is that everyone here in the village owes him their lives. Me," she paused as she looked at Clarice, "and her included."

That's the same thing the stewardess said.

He looked over and they made eye contact. But only for a moment before she smiled and nodded her head to signal for him to look the other way. He turned and saw two men coming from one of the larger homes.

One was Killian.

He and an old man stood outside the door. The expressions they wore were serious, but their attention was quickly diverted when two young boys ran up to Killian and started babbling on. Whatever they had said, it looked like Killian had surrendered and agreed to it.

Hawke's eyes widened as Killian smiled, and the boys each grabbed an arm. He lifted them; their feet dangled off the ground. The boys laughed and swung as Killian's laughter melted with theirs.

It was something he didn't think was possible. It was as if the man he read about and the man he saw now were two completely different people.

Killian's eyes caught Hawke's as he glanced over. His joy melted as he returned to his trademark stoic expression. He let the boys down and sent them on their way as they continued to laugh. He then excused himself from the elder and started towards Hawke and Clarice.

"There are a lot of things you don't know about Mr. Blackwell."

Hawke's attention went back to Clarice, who then proceeded to take the now-sleeping child from his arm. She coddled her softly, like a mother holding her own child. She bowed her head slightly as she walked past. "There are a lot of things you don't know about us either," she stated. "But I hope you'll give us all a chance." And with that, Clarice made her way to the house two doors down and went inside.

Hawke stood frozen for a moment.

What's going on with these people?

He couldn't wrap his head around it.

As if on cue to his internal screams, Killian's hand rested on his shoulder. The pure irritation he felt from not being able to understand the situation started to bubble out. He shrugged off Killian's hand and made his way inside the house.

Killian paused but said nothing. He felt like Hawke's thick-headed attitude was going to be a pain this whole trip but tried not to think about it too much. A small sigh escaped as he also made his way inside.

Though the house was small, it felt rather homey.

A mudroom welcomed guests to remove their shoes before entering the kitchen. A small table with a ragged tablecloth and two seats sat to the left, as a large plaster stove was across the room. It was like the pizza ovens Hawke knew from New York and made him feel a bit nostalgic. Beneath the stove sat a small stack of wood, which was to be used to heat the house.

To the right of the furnace were a small door and an opening. The door on the left led to the bedroom, which housed two queen beds on either side with a small nightstand between them. A decent-sized mirror hung on the opposite wall, which helped spread light around the room. The opening on the right led to a small living room, which housed a small loveseat pushed against the left wall and a long table and two chairs to the right. Small bulbs hung from simple cords throughout the house as sunlight poured in from the opened shades on the windows. Or, what would have been windows if there were glass on them. Instead, they were just openings in the wall that could be closed off with the shutters.

Hawke took in the ambiance as he placed his bag on the table in the living room.

"Cozy," he muttered under his breath.

Killian went around to the other side of the table and followed suit, setting his own bag down as well. "I like to think it is," he stated. "Did you think you would be living in the lap of luxury while we were here?" his question oozed with sarcasm as he moseyed over to the couch and sat down.

Hawke's irritation was growing more and more by the minute. "No," he stated as he turned around to face him. "Why would I think a rat would live in luxury regardless of where they go?"

Killian's eye twitched at Hawke's remark, but he wasn't going to let him win this. "You're right," he stated as he shrugged. "I couldn't expect a bird brain like you to understand the joys of simple living."

Their eyes met as Hawke growled, "I'll show you, bird brain," and made his way around the table.

"You're already doing a wonderful job," Killian taunted as he stood back up and moved towards his adversary.

They met at the end of the table as they grabbed one another by the collar of their shirts. The tension was so thick it could've been cut with a knife.

Silence deafened the room for a few moments before Killian scoffed and pushed Hawke away as he released his shirt. "This isn't worth it," he mumbled as he used his other hand to push back the hair that had fallen on his face.

Hawke didn't fight back but instead copied Killian and let go. "At least that's one thing we can agree on," he stated as he pushed past Killian, purposely hitting his shoulder with his own. He sat down on the small couch and, in one fluid motion, put his arms behind his head, lay back on the arm, and closed his eyes. "I'm exhausted, so I'm gonna rest for a bit before we go scouting," he paused as he opened one eye. "As long as you're ok with that, *fearless leader*." The pure mockery of his tone was comical.

Killian scoffed as he turned and made his way to the bedroom. "Do whatever you want," he stated, "just be sure not to wet the couch." He paused before he went out of sight. "I don't have any puppy pads handy."

It took every bit of resistance and self-control Hawke had for him not to get up and beat the living shit out of him. Truthfully, the only reason he didn't was because his exhaustion was stronger than his anger. He almost growled as he rolled over and drifted off to sleep.

"Stupid mutt," Killian muttered under his breath as he entered the bedroom and plopped down on the bed closest to him. It had been a long time since he'd worked alongside someone, especially someone who didn't fear him and was on par with his own strength and smarts.

Don't think I've worked with anyone this fucking annoying either.

His thoughts vented as he leaned back and rested his head on the small pillow. It took no time at all before his eyes fluttered shut and he too drifted off to dreamland.

"Mom?"

A young boy with brown hair and eyes called out in complete darkness.

"MOM!?"

His voice cracked from his broken scream.

He walked but then jolted into a sprint.

Tears flowed from his eyes as he continued to call out.

"Mom! Mooooom! Momma!?"

He slowed down.

"Mommy?" He asked, his voice barely a whisper as tears dripped from his cheeks.

Suddenly, a small light appeared in the distance, accentuating the body of a woman.

The joy on the boy's face radiated as he darted towards it.

"Mom!" His tone now brimmed with happiness and hope.

He drew closer.

And closer.

And closer.

But never close enough.

The figure stayed distant no matter how far he ran. He reached out his hand in hopes of reaching her.

"MOM!"

Without warning, the woman's body shifted. As if by magic, the boy stood beside her but was met with horror. Her skin was cut and mangled as blood covered her hair, hands, and face. Her eyes were solid white, devoid of life.

Although he wanted to run, he couldn't move.

He was frozen in place.

He could do nothing as the terrifying monster leaned in close and whispered in his ear, "Killian."

Killian shot up as cold sweat covered his face. His breathing was ragged, and his eyes wide as he looked around. It took a few seconds, but once he realized where he was, he calmed himself down and slowed his breathing. He then placed his hand on his head and clenched his teeth.

"Why now?" He whispered to himself. It had been ages since he'd had such a vivid nightmare.

"Whatcha doing?"

His eyes peeked through his fingers as he looked up and saw Hawke leaning against the doorway. A rather long sigh escaped his lips as he put his hand down and got up from the bed.

"It's none of your business," he stated as he pushed past Hawke. "Let's get going. We need to survey the area."

Hawke allowed the push, but not because he was intimidated. Although his expression remained stoic, internally, he felt what could have been called sympathy. He knew what it was like to live with demons that haunted your dreams. It was something he had dealt with for a very long time.

"A'right," Hawke agreed nonchalantly as he followed him to the living room.

Without another word, they went into their bags and gathered a few necessities. They both picked one of their handguns and two magazines of ammo. Hawke situated his in the back of his pants with a small holster, while Killian's holster was down his thigh. Their choice of locations was about as different as they were.

The fact that Killian grabbed a switchblade while Hawke grabbed a pair of brass knuckles made it even more evident.

"Let's get going," Killian stated as he headed towards the door.

Hawke didn't respond but followed nonetheless.

It wasn't until they got outside that Hawke decided to ask a rather important question.

"Where we headed?" His question was justified. He knew nothing of this area, and anything that could help him get his bearings faster would be helpful.

Killian continued through town while he spoke. "We're heading towards the treeline where one of the boys found the blood-covered toy."

There was a moment of pause.

"And the toy belonged to his brother, who went missing."

Hawke's expression changed. He read about that in the file, but to hear it out loud felt different.

It was obvious he felt sorry for the boy. He could only imagine what would happen if his younger sister went missing like that. He would have burned the whole forest down looking for her.

"Then we'd better find him," Hawke stated as he caught up.

Killian looked over and, for the first time since this mission began, he agreed with a nod.

They needed to find the boy.

Or at least provide closure for the family.

5

Forest Time

It didn't take them long to hit the tree line and become engulfed in the eerily peaceful forest outside the village.

Hawke admired the simple beauty of the trees and rays of sunlight that broke through their leaves.

"If I were here for any other reason than this, I feel like I could enjoy this view a lot more," Hawke stated as he followed Killian through the maze of nature.

"It is beautiful this time of the year," Killian responded. "Although I prefer the wintertime when the snow covers the landscape in an untouched blanket. There's something eerily peaceful about it."

Hawke could imagine the silence and serene snow-covered hills.

RUSTLE! RUSTLE!

Killian stopped abruptly, which caused Hawke to bump into him.

"What the fuck are you…" Hawke's words were cut short as Killian raised his fist beside his head and placed his other finger over his mouth.

Hawke's instincts and training kicked in as he realized what Killian was saying.

They were being watched.

Killian motioned forward with a point, and they continued. However, the atmosphere around them was very different.

Although it seemed they were the ones being followed, their eyes bore a predatory gaze as they surveyed their surroundings.

"DUCK!" Killian yelled as he grabbed Hawke by the front of his shirt and pulled them down together.

Hawke's eyes followed a blur that had gone past where his head was a second ago.

His eyes focused on the dagger stuck in the tree behind him. His muscles tightened as they stood back up and saw the culprit.

The masked man turned and tried to run.

"Not so fast!" Hawke yelled as he darted and tackled their assailant.

Killian moved with the intention to help but was cut short. Two more men came from behind the surrounding trees with knives drawn. As one lunged forward, Killian grabbed the assailant's wrist and, using his own momentum, caused him to fall to the ground. The other man followed behind and came closer than his friend, which caused Killian to get a small cut on his face from the blade.

As he dodged, the first man was back up and coming from behind. Through instinct, Killian grabbed the wrist of the one in front and lunged it into the chest of the one behind. He then grabbed the blade from the second man and quickly plunged it between the eyes of the other. Both men fell to the ground instantly.

"You could have left them alive, you know," Hawke stated as he came up beside him.

Killian met his gaze before he looked over and saw the original assailant lying unconscious.

"Filth doesn't deserve to live." The lack of emotion behind his words was concerning. "We have one alive to question. That's enough."

Hawke couldn't help but pause. He had thought maybe the file was wrong and Killian wasn't a heartless murdering monster, but it seemed he was the one in the wrong. "You're one sick son of a-"

Five more men came from the trees and surrounded them. They instinctively turned in opposite directions, their backs pressed against each other.

"Guess this is the only time I'm glad to have a Viper on my side," Hawke remarked as he side-eyed Killian. "Just try not to get in my way."

Killian smirked and said, "Same goes for you, Wendigo."

They both smiled as the enemies attacked.

Hawke defended against the two attacking him, quickly bringing them down as he dodged their rookie stabs and punched them hard to render them unconscious.

Killian, on the other hand, did not.

As one lunged at him with their dagger, he dodged and grabbed their neck.

SNAP!

The man fell to the ground. He took the knife from his victim as he dodged the second assailant.

Within seconds, he turned back and slit the man's throat. He gargled for a few seconds before he fell and joined the first one.

The last man standing looked on in horror as he witnessed the almost elegant way his buddies were dispatched.

"You're going to tell us who sent you," Hawke stated, cracking his knuckles in sync with his words.

The man appeared to be readying himself for a brawl, but then swiftly turned and ran deeper into the forest.

Hawke and Killian stood for a second before they both let out an irritated sigh and gave chase. They bobbed and weaved through the large trees before the man came to a river and seemed to trip on some of the rocks below the waterline.

"He's mine!" Hawke stated as he ran into the river and straddled their enemy. He threw punch after punch at the man's face, but very few made contact as his punches were blocked.

"Well, this won't do," Hawke announced as he quickly stood up and grabbed the man by the collar. The pull-up disoriented the assailant long enough for...

PUNCH!

Hawke landed a blow to his jaw. However, the water and a smooth rock below his foot caused him to slip. They both stumbled, but his opponent regained his composure a second before he did. That split second was long enough for the man to run forward, grab Hawke by the waist, and plow him into one of the large tree trunks off the bank.

THUD!

Pain shot through Hawke's back as he gasped for the air knocked from his lungs.

As if his instincts took over, he lifted his linked hands and brought them down hard on the enemy's back. The man fell to the ground but rolled to the side and avoided the low kick Hawke had tried to land.

Hawke then tried to land another punch, but his opponent scooped up dirt and sand towards his face. Unfortunately, he couldn't react fast enough, and some landed in his eyes.

As Hawke tried to get his sight back, his opponent caught sight of a small glimmer shining below the water. It seemed that during their fight, Hawke's gun had fallen into the water. With a rather twisted smile, his enemy quickly waded through the current and grabbed it for himself.

Hawke was finally able to open one of his eyes, but by that time, it was too late.

All he saw was their enemy pointing his own gun at him, ready to fire.

There was no time left.

BANG!

No one moved as the birds who once rested in the treetops scattered above to the winds. The sound of the river cascading over its rock bed and the occasional rustle of the brush was joined by the splash of a gun hitting the water.

Hawke stood motionless as he waited for the pain to set in.

But it didn't.

In fact, apart from the irritation in his eyes, there was nothing wrong with him.

No blood.

No pain.

Nothing.

The other man, however, was not so lucky.

SPLASH!

His body lay motionless as the current carried his blood downstream.

Hawke cleaned out his other eye quickly, then looked behind him.

There, with a gun in hand, stood Killian on the riverbank.

His stance was almost mesmerizing.

The pure menace in his eyes and the strength behind his dominating pose were intimidating even for Hawke.

Killian, after seeing the blood drift past him, relaxed his arm and breathed a sigh of relief. He held the gun to his side as he looked to Hawke and smirked.

"You can pay me back with a drink later."

Hawke scoffed, then snickered. "I guess I do owe ya one for that," he stated as he waded through the water and emerged on the other side. He stood in front of Killian and, with a sincere smile, extended his hand as he said, "Thanks."

Although Hawke was a stubborn man, he sincerely believed that one's actions spoke louder than any words. The fact that Killian had shot the enemy before the enemy shot him made Hawke feel like he could somewhat trust him.

Even if it was just a little bit.

His gesture took Killian by surprise. The last thing he thought he would ever hear from him was a thank you.

But he was going to take it.

There was still a mission to complete, and even though they were like oil and water, it couldn't hurt to get along a little better while they were there. With his own smile, he reached for his hand and said, "No problem."

BANG!

They both paused.

Their hands only inches apart.

Killian looked down and, using his once outstretched hand, touched his chest. Dread covered his face as he looked and saw his fingertips saturated in blood.

Hawke could see the blood spreading through his shirt as the realization hit them both.

He'd been shot.

COUGH!

Blood spewed from Killian's mouth as he dropped his gun and fell to his knees. Hawke instantly knelt to his level, trying to keep him from falling over completely. "Killian! You have ta stay awake, ya can't —"

STING!

"Ow!" Hawke winced as he looked to his thigh and saw a dart.

Shit.

Instantly, his body went limp, and they both fell to the ground.

Men in the same uniforms as those they just fought spawned from every crevice of the forest. Hawke couldn't move or say anything as a few of them came with a stretcher and rather forcefully threw Killian on it. He screamed in pain but was ignored. His blood seeped into the once white fabric of the gurney as they took him away.

Hawke wanted to stop them, but he couldn't.

Whatever they had used was strong, even for him. As he struggled to move, one man walked up and crouched down beside him. He rested a sniper rifle on his shoulder as he used his other hand to grab Hawke's chin to make their eyes meet.

Nothing was said, but he could tell this man was a killer. There was no soul behind those dark auburn eyes.

"Take them both," the enemy stated as he released Hawke's face. "I'm sure we can find a use for this one."

You son of a bitch!

Hawke's thought barely finished before the butt of the man's gun rammed into his face and knocked him unconscious.

6

Laboratory

"Mom?" A small boy with black hair and blue eyes walked through the darkness as he clenched his hands around his arms.

What sounded like static from an old TV came from behind him.

When he turned, the sound stopped, but a casket rested beneath a solitary light with a blacked-out figure sitting inside.

His face saddened as he walked closer.

"Mom?"

He reached the casket, and the light died down. Once he was able to make out the being before him, he couldn't say a word.

Horror covered his face.

A corpse with decayed flesh and blood falling from the bones sat in the once pristine casket. The monster smiled as it leaned towards the frozen young boy. Its tone was raspy and bone-chilling as it said, "Mommy loves you."

Hawke's eyes shot open as a gasp escaped his lips and sweat rolled down his forehead.

It was a dream.

He let out a sigh of relief, but when he tried to wipe the sweat from his brow, he was greeted with resistance. Looking over, his wrists were shackled to a concrete wall. He tugged on the chains once or twice before letting out an aggravated sigh, which matched the irritated tone as he mumbled, "Great..."

Looking down, he was wearing sweatpants and a plain white t-shirt. Definitely not the clothes he'd been wearing when they were attacked.

"Where the hell....?"

As he pushed himself up against the wall, it didn't take him long to realize where he was.

A prison cell.

Though the layout was similar, the size was not your typical jail cell. It was almost the size of his first apartment. Seemed like overkill in his opinion. It had the traditional items inside: a sink with a small mirror above it, the bed, and the toilet. All of which looked like they hadn't been cleaned in a very long time.

Let's hope I don't have to use the bathroom any time soon.

However, the comical thought was quickly replaced by a serious one.

Bet we'll find the kids here.

His mind raced as he looked past the bars and noticed a small table and chair to the far right of the room. A few small incandescent bulbs spread out on the ceiling were the only light source.

There were no windows and only one door.

He continued to analyze the room before the lock on the door clicked and opened. A rather tall woman strolled in with her hands resting in the pockets of her lab coat. The smug look she wore instantly put Hawke on high alert.

"So do you like your new cage, my little birdie?" Her American accent took Hawke by surprise, but he didn't show it.

He needed to figure out what the hell was going on before he delved into her family tree.

Slim glasses hugged her face but complemented the curvature of her cheeks. Her long brown hair was pulled back into a loose ponytail with a few strands loosely sitting on her shoulders.

There was something about her, though.

Something that was giving Hawke the heebie-jeebies.

Deciding to see if he could get some information from her, Hawke smirked as he lifted one of his hands and shook it, making the attached chain jingle. "The least you could've done was make them furry handcuffs so I wouldn't have to worry about bruising later."

The woman's expression remained unreadable as she snickered under her breath. "I will take that into consideration next time I have a guest." As she spoke, she took a set of keys from her coat and unlocked the prison door. It squeaked slowly as she made her way inside.

Just a little closer.

It was all he needed to grab her.

Unfortunately, it looked like she knew exactly how long his chains were.

With an irritated sigh at his defeat, Hawke made his way closer. The chains rattled until he stopped inches from his gracious host. Though he continued to wear his unbothered expression, his patience was running thin.

The woman smiled. She even leaned forward, just enough to be face-to-face with him. "What's wrong, little birdie? Have your wings been clipped so you can no longer fly?"

Her sing-song tone sent Hawke over the edge.

He pulled and pulled against the cuffs, trying his best to grab her, until his wrists became raw and small trails of blood flowed down his arms.

The woman did nothing but stand there. "Seems like you're in the perfect condition for my next experiment."

Hawke paused, then slowly backed away. He cocked his brow and looked rather unamused. "What experiment?"

"Oh, don't worry," the woman said as she turned and walked back outside the cell. "You'll know soon enough."

Without missing a beat, the door opened again. This time, however, it was thrown open and slammed against the wall. Two men in the same gear as before plowed into the cell, followed by a younger scientist with a small computer.

Hawke was ready to fight until he saw what the soldiers were carrying.

"Killian?!" he yelled as the limp body they were dragging was thrown to the ground in front of him. His clothes had also been changed.

Hawke's internal voice was screaming.

I have a bad feeling about this.

The two men turned and left the room with the woman following behind. However, she stopped at the door and looked back. "Have fun, my little birdie." The sinister tone was only complemented by the maniacal laugh he heard after she shut the door.

After a moment passed and the crazy broad's laugh vanished, Hawke ticked his jaw in anger and redirected his attention. "Killian!"

There was no movement.

"KILLIAN!"

His finger twitched.

Slowly, he moved and pushed up to rest on all fours. He shook his head to try to get the ringing in his ears to stop. "What the..", he muttered as he looked up and saw Hawke, which snapped him back to reality.

However, when he pushed himself up to rest on his knees, he became dizzy and fell back to land on his behind. "Owww."

The pure relief Hawke felt from seeing him alive was…

Alive?

Wait a second!

"How are you alive?! You were as good as dead when that sniper shot you!"

Killian rubbed his temple as he looked at Hawke. "Must you be so loud? I am right HERE!", he yelled the last word to bring his point home. "And I don't know. Obviously, I didn't die, or I wouldn't be here." The obvious sarcasm dripping from his last few words made Hawke cock his brow.

It was Killian, but it wasn't.

His demeanor was different.

"Then how else do you explain getting shot in the chest and dying your shirt from the blood seeping from said wound? Those are kind of DEAD", being sure to enunciate, "giveaways after all."

Without meaning to, Killian couldn't help but snicker. "Well, apparently your assessment was...." his voice stopped as he sniffed the air. He smelled something. It was something he couldn't put his finger on, but it smelled....

Delicious.

"Do you smell that?" He followed his nose until it seemed like it was coming from somewhere near Hawke.

"Smell what?" As if to make sure it wasn't him, Hawke smelled his own underarm and was pleasantly surprised to see that he was well-groomed for a prisoner.

"How can you not smell...that..." Killian's voice trailed off as he figured out the smell's origin. Beautiful raindrops of blood hit the floor beneath Hawke's arms. Each drip seemed to mesmerize him.

BA-THUMP

His head started to pulsate.

He grabbed both sides of his temple but couldn't stop the pain. It was like hammers were being smashed against his skull. Unable to keep the pain inside, he released a gut-wrenching scream as he fell backwards on the floor.

"Killian!" Hawke yelled as he tried to snap him out of whatever was happening. "Killian! What's going on!?" As he tried to grab his attention, he noticed something was happening to him. His hair started to lighten. It was as if the color itself was bleeding away.

"I...don't know."

Killian could barely speak between his clenched teeth. Another scream filled the cell as the pulsating got worse with each second. "Make....it stop!"

He wanted it to stop.

Anything to make this pain stop!

Another pulse went through his skull, but this one was different.

The screaming stopped as his arms relaxed beside him.

He was motionless.

"Killian?"

Hawke couldn't see his face.

Saying nothing, Killian slowly pushed himself up and stood slouched forward.

Hawke's body tensed. It was as if his body sensed something he couldn't.

"Kill," he started to call for him again, but was cut off as Killian almost teleported from where he stood to right in front of him.

When did he!?

They stood face to face for a moment before Hawke noticed another change in his appearance.

His eyes had changed color.

The once soft brown was replaced with a disturbing blood red.

"What happened to your...."

His question was cut short as Killian's hand wrapped around his neck, cutting off his airway. Hawke gasped for air as he grabbed his wrist and tried to pry it off.

It was no use.

It was like a python had wrapped itself around him.

As he struggled, Killian's eyes drifted to the small trails of blood painting his arms.

With methodical and predator-like grace, Killian leaned in and sniffed the streaks slowly. The smell was intoxicating. It was as if desire itself had manifested in a physical form.

As he was drawn to sample this mesmerizing delicacy, he leaned in and opened his mouth. It was then that one could see his canines had grown. Only slightly, but enough to accentuate the small drops of fluid coming from their tips.

It was like a viper oozing with venom.

"Delicious..."

The sheer animalistic tone sent shivers down Hawke's spine.

He extended his tongue and slowly licked a small patch of blood from his elbow. When it hit his tongue, his eyes widened and his pupils dilated.

The taste was...

Orgasmic.

His vision blurred as immense hunger swept through him. Saliva dripped from his mouth, and his body tensed. This time, he quickly leaned in and bit into Hawke's arm.

The magnificent taste of blood rushed into his mouth and sent a wave of euphoria rushing through him. It was something that words couldn't describe as he shut his eyes to bask in the feeling. With each gulp, it intensified, but it wasn't the same for Hawke.

"AAHHHH!"

Ear piercing screams echoed through the cell.

He was in so much pain. It felt as though electric shocks fried every nerve and muscle in his body.

It was agonizing at first, but after a few seconds, it changed.

A feeling of peace rushed over him. His body was numb, and his mind was empty. His eyes glazed over as he lost his last bit of strength.

One final thought raced through his mind...

I'm going to die.

Then everything went black.

Killian opened his eyes as he released Hawke's arm and leaned back.

However, once he did, he was greeted with the horrible sight.

His eyes widened as he saw Hawke's limp body underneath his grip. He released him instantly as he took a step back.

The body fell with a thud and lay still.

He looked down at his hand and couldn't figure out what happened. He remembered being thrown into the cell and then talking to Hawke. Then the pulsating pain rushed through his head and then...

His thoughts paused as he felt something wet on the corner of his mouth. He used his thumb to wipe it off and was horrified when he saw what it was.

Blood.

"What?" his voice trembled as his hands began to shake. His eyes darted to Hawke, who still lay motionless.

It was then that he realized what had happened.

Hawke was dead, and it was all his fault.

7

Escape

His strength vanished as he collapsed to his knees. Killian could do nothing. His eyes glanced from Hawke to his blood-stained hands.

"What did they do...to me?" The sheer terror in his voice was humbling.

His mind raced as his sanity began to slip.

He didn't even notice Hawke twitch as he woke up.

Hawke blinked a time or two as he pushed himself up slowly. His eyes took a second to refocus as he realized Killian was sitting in front of him. Instinctively, he pushed himself back.

His breathing was ragged and strained as he hit the wall. The small jolt knocked him back into reality, which helped him realize something wasn't right. He lifted his arm and looked for the puncture marks.

He had to get them closed as soon as possible, or he would...

"Wait," he softly mumbled.

He examined the bottom of his elbow closely but could see no blood. The only bit left was the remnants of the damage to his wrist.

It was then he saw two small scars where Killian had fed.

"What the hell," he responded as he then examined his wrists.

Minus the scarring, they were healed too.

"What the fuck?" he whispered as he turned his attention back to his cellmate.

His hair and eyes were still the same off-putting colors as before. However, what concerned him the most was the growing insanity behind those eyes.

He gritted his teeth and reached forward to place his shaking hand on Killian's shoulder.

The touch Killian felt made him turn around instantly. His eyes were wide as he saw it was Hawke.

He broke a small smile, but it vanished when the blood on Hawke's arm reminded him of what he'd done. Quickly, he pushed himself up and back towards the other side of the cell. He stopped beside the sink, unable to face him.

Hawke's own hand hovered for a moment before he formed a fist and brought it to rest at his side. He said nothing as he stared at Killian.

The silence was deafening.

"I'm sorry", Killian whispered in shame.

Struggling to get back to his feet due to his weakened state, Hawke leaned against the wall and shifted upwards.

"It's not your fault."

Just getting up felt like he'd run a marathon.

"It's those bastards that caused this."

Killian turned to face Hawke but stopped when he caught sight of himself in the mirror above the sink. His eyes remained locked as he got closer. He then took his hand and pulled down on his cheek a bit to expose his eye. He noticed their color change matched the blood stains on his cheek.

Then he noticed his fangs and hair.

He pulled up slightly on his lip and stared at his pointed canines. Afterwards, he pulled softly on a piece of hair to make sure it was actually his. Unfortunately, it was.

It was then that the realization hit him.

He'd been turned into a monster.

A villain from a fairy tale.

A disgusting monstrosity.

He grabbed the sink to hold himself up as he resisted the urge to puke.

"What the hell DID they do to me?", he muttered under his breath as his grip tightened. He clenched his teeth as his anger grew until he yelled in rage and slammed his fist down.

THUD!

The front half of the sink hit the concrete floor, shattering into smaller pieces.

Both stared in disbelief.

Hawke broke the silence with the jingle of his chains as he adjusted his stance. "Killian, you need to stay calm," he said.

Looking down at his hands, Killian resisted every urge he had to scream.

What the fuck is going on!?

Thoughts ran through his mind as he struggled to contain his emotions. He couldn't control anything anymore.

Not his hunger.

Not his emotions.

Nothing.

Everything he had fought and trained for was gone.

Now he was nothing more than a freak of nature.

A rejected science experiment.

"I....I," he stuttered as he started to spiral again.

"Killian!" Hawke shouted as his knees buckled and he almost fell back to the floor.

Killian jolted back to reality and slowly looked over to Hawke. Taking a deep breath to calm his mind, he stood up straight and wiped the blood from his face. He said nothing as he walked over and stood a few feet from Hawke.

Though he tried, Hawke couldn't hide how terrified he was.

Who could blame him, though?

He had literally been sucked dry by a… monster who was trapped in the same cage. Anyone would have been terrified.

Gritting his teeth before he spoke, Killian looked to the side. "I'm sorry for what I did to you, but we need to get out of here." He was trying to contain his raw emotions the best he could.

But it was damn near impossible.

Killian wasn't sure how long he could keep them in check, so they needed to escape.

And fast.

Especially considering just the residual smell of blood on Hawke's arms was enough to drive him to the brink.

Hawke thought for a moment. His strength was slowly returning, but it would be a while before he could walk, let alone run. As he let out a sigh, he could see how hard Killian was fighting against his new carnal urges.

They would tackle that conundrum later, but right now they needed to escape.

"I agree," he stated as he looked around the cell, "but how do you intend for us to get out of this cell? Let alone, wherever the fuck this cell is with how weak I am."

It seemed like both of them were at their wits' end.

And for understandable reasons.

First, they got kidnapped.

Then one was turned into a blood sucking monster who decided to use the other as an all-you-can-eat buffet.

This mission was turning out to be fantastic.

"I think I can handle that."

Killian looked down at his palms, then clenched his fists as he moved closer.

"Just hold still."

He reached over slowly and grabbed one of the cuffs with both hands. As he exhaled, he pulled with all his might.

SNAP!

The cuff swung down and chimed as it collided with the wall.

Hawke's eyes were wide with disbelief. He just broke a solid metal cuff with his bare hands. The weight of their situation was really starting to set in.

Saying nothing, Killian broke the other cuff.

As he rubbed his wrists, Hawke then watched as Killian made his way to the cell door.

The man he had read about in the file was gone.

What was left was a monster that could snap his neck like a twig.

A shiver went down his spine as he thought about the next time Killian went into a feeding frenzy.

He just hoped he wouldn't be the main course.

CLANK!

The lock on the door skidded across the floor until it stopped only inches from Hawke.

"I opened the gate," Killian said as he turned and made his way back over. However, when he did, he turned and knelt with his back towards Hawke. "Now get on."

There was a moment of silence.

"You can't be serious...", Hawke said with a rather unamused tone.

Irritated, Killian looked back. "If you have a better idea, I'd love to hear it!"

Hawke thought for a moment but couldn't come up with anything. Letting out a deep sigh, he pushed his body from the wall and mounted Killian.

Expecting to feel Hawke's weight, Killian stood up slowly.

"What the...," he said in disbelief. He weighed practically nothing. It felt like he was carrying a stuffed animal instead of a full-grown man.

Hawke didn't really care why Killian seemed rather surprised. Although he wanted this joyride to be over as soon as possible, he couldn't resist the urge to have a bit of fun. He tapped his feet against Killian's side and said, "Giddy-up, horsey."

Killian said nothing but couldn't help but smirk. It was rather funny to see the big, bad Hawke acting like a kid on his back.

Nothing else was said as Killian walked out of the cell and stopped in front of the door. As he slowly turned the knob, he realized it wasn't locked and opened it. This sent a sense of dread over him.

Their day had already started badly, and he had a feeling it was only going to get worse.

8

Experiments

When Killian peeked outside, he was rather surprised to see they were underground in dark, hand-carved tunnels. Although he had no idea of their current location, Killian wasted no time surveying the hall to the left, then right.

Luckily, there was no one around.

Which was great considering neither one of them was in any shape to fight.

They emerged from the room and quietly shut the door.

However, they were only steps away before they weren't alone.

Muttering voices were heard down a small hallway to the left and were progressively getting louder.

They needed to find a place to hide and fast. Killian looked around and saw the door to their right was partially cracked.

He made his way inside.

To not make a sound, he grabbed the doorknob and turned it slowly as the door shut. After the door was closed, he peeked through the blinds.

The voices grew louder until they were just outside. They appeared to be doctors discussing notes. It seemed like they hadn't noticed anything strange and continued until their voices vanished down the halls.

As Killian let go of the blinds and let out his held breath, Hawke spotted something from the corner of his eye. He turned his head and almost gagged at what he saw in the dimly lit room. He blamed his weakened state, but even the strongest man's stomach would've turned.

Killian also realized something was wrong when his adrenaline calmed, and he started to smell the magnificent scent of blood again.

Although this time it wasn't Hawke's.

He turned, and his eyes grew wide, joining Hawke in his expression of disgust.

In front of them lay the body of a small boy attached to an operating table. His organs sat in jars on either side while his skull remained intact, with only the skin pulled away. Vials of blood-filled beakers covered a small table to the side. Although it seemed most of the blood had been removed, some dripped from the side and tapped the floor beneath the table.

Hawke slowly dismounted. "Who could do such a thing?" he asked as he slowly walked towards the poor kid.

Killian, however, couldn't move.

The smell of blood was even more concentrated here than it was in the cell. It took everything he had to stop his body from leaning down and licking the floor.

He was disgusted with himself.

To distract from the hunger, he walked to the other side of the bed and examined the corpse. "Whoever did this was a professional. All the organs were removed perfectly intact and with minimal damage to the inside."

"Thanks, Dr," Hawke responded with a slightly sarcastic tone. "It's not like a lab would have professionals or anything."

Killian glared as he looked up, but Hawke had already made his way to the end of the table. He had planned on making a smart remark back, but stopped when he noticed Hawke's expression darkened.

"What is it?" he asked.

"I just realized this is probably one of the boys that went missing from the village," Hawke stated as he stared at the corpse.

Killian's eyes grew wide as he looked at the exposed skull.

"The similarities between him and the other children are almost uncanny."

BANG!

Killian pounded his hand on the wall behind him as he clenched his fist. "Damnit!" The crumbled rocks from the wall pattered softly on the floor.

Hawke took in a deep breath as he turned and found stacks of paperwork strewn across the counter. His agent instincts kicked in, and he quickly went to work. "Hey," he said to get Killian's attention. "Come look at this."

Killian made his way over and took the papers from Hawke. Using the lamp above the corpse, he glanced over them.

"It looks like they've been running experiments on humans for a while now," Killian summarized as he continued to read. "Seems they've been trying to perfect a bio-weapon of some kind." He couldn't find any details, though. It seemed most of those had been blacked out or omitted.

"Most of their subjects have been failures, though," Hawke stated. "Here's a list of what happened to the most recent patients." He offered a small handwritten note.

As he read, a knot formed in the pit of Killian's stomach.

Lizard: Removed limbs to see if they grew back - FAILURE

Owl: Exposed them to bright lights to test their vision sensitivity - FAILURE

Honey Badger: Injected with poison to test resistance - FAILURE

Killian crumpled the paper in his hand. "What kind of sick bastards are we dealing with?"

"I don't know, but it seems like this mission just got a lot more complicated."

Killian then noticed a small laptop sitting on the edge of the counter. He decided to see what else he could find as he made his way over.

"Hey," Hawke stated. "What are you doing?"

"I'm going to see what else these bastards are doing," he said as he began hacking into the system.

Hawke couldn't help but stare in amazement. "Is there anything you're *not* good at?

Killian snickered before a small ding came from the computer. "Bingo!" He'd found the patient files. As he glanced through, anger boiled up inside. He continued until one file caught his attention. His eyes raced side to side as he looked it over, but he didn't finish. In fact, his eyes stopped suddenly, and without a word, he turned and walked away.

Hawke didn't want to, but he needed to see what caused Killian to have that reaction. And honestly, he wished he hadn't.

It seemed they were in a lab commissioned to create genetically mutated humans as weapons of war. The base for the weapon was to turn a person into a flesh-eating monstrosity who eventually died on their own by the insatiable hunger they felt. Although the documents went into the cost of testing and supplies, it didn't disclose who the guarantor was, but whoever it was must have been loaded.

The project had been going on for years.

Hawke's stomach sank at the thought. How many people had been kidnapped and used as guinea pigs before now?

As Hawke continued scanning the files, Killian tried to calm down. His anger was boiling, and due to whatever the hell they'd done to him, he couldn't control it.

He wanted to break things.

"What does the rest of the file say?" Killian asked between clenched teeth as he tried to breathe.

Hawke said nothing.

Killian looked over his shoulder with his eyebrow raised. "Hawke?"

Hawke's face made it obvious that whatever it said was not good.

"I found the last file," he stated, "and it's about you."

Killian's eyes shot open as he made his way back to the monitor, almost pushing Hawke out of his way. He read through the general notes until he got to the last line, which made the air leave his lungs.

It read…

TEST SUBJECT Z: VARIANT FOUND

Hawke watched as so many emotions ran across Killian's face. He said nothing, but suddenly a look of horror broke his stoic expression as what appeared to be black blood began to seep from the corners of Killian's eyes.

They needed to get out of there.

Immediately.

"Killian," he said as he placed his hand on his shoulder. "We need to go."

With a small sigh and a deep breath, Killian regained his composure and turned off the computer as he wiped his eyes clean. "You're right," he stated and walked to stand beside the corpse. "We need to find a way out, but we also need to see if there are any survivors."

"What are you talking about?!" Hawke questioned before he closed the distance and grabbed him by the collar of his shirt. "For all we know, they've already been turned into the real-life version of Operation, like the kid here!"

"You might be right," Killian emotionlessly responded. "We have to see what we can find, though." He grabbed Hawke by the wrist and rather forcefully made him release his grip. "I will not leave without making sure there is no one left to save."

Hawke winced as the grip on his wrist made his hand pulsate. He pulled away quickly and rubbed it as he sighed. "Damnit!"

There was no denying he was against this idea, but it's not like he could argue and win at the moment.

"Fine. I saw in the files where they keep the prisoners. We'll try there." He looked back to meet Killian's eyes. "If there are no survivors, we leave immediately. Agreed?"

"Agreed," Killian stated as he knelt, and Hawke mounted. "Where did it say I needed to go?"

Hawke paused as he went through the information in his head. His photographic memory was a definite plus in this kind of situation. "It said Section C. If I remember, I saw a B on the far side of the wall here."

Killian nodded before he peeked through the blinds and, after making sure the coast was clear, opened the door. They darted down the hallway until they spotted a C painted on the opposite wall.

They were close.

Something was off, though.

Killian noticed he could hear things better than before. He heard people talking in the labs, but it wasn't just muffles. He could hear their words as if they were standing right beside him. Before he had a chance to really think about it, though, they had to dart down a side hall to avoid a group coming towards them.

Luckily, it was the spot they needed to be in anyway.

A large number of cells lined the hallway, each one smaller than a half-bath and filled with three to four people. Most of the prisoners were already dead or knocking on death's door. They were sitting in their own waste, and their bones showed through their skin. Their eyes were glazed over, and it seemed all hope of returning home had left them.

It was disgusting.

Killian stopped a few cells down as Hawke dismounted. They stood in silence as their anger grew with every step they took.

"We couldn't have saved all of them," Killian said out loud as if to reassure himself that this was not their fault.

Hawke clenched his fists as he followed.

"I know."

"Killian," Hawke stated as he stopped in front of a cell.

Killian turned and looked inside.

A younger boy was sitting between the corpses of his cellmates, which appeared to have been dead for quite a while. The life behind his eyes was strong, even though his body was nothing more than skin and bones.

"I know this boy," Killian stated. "He's Nikolai, the grandson of the village elder." As he spoke, he grabbed the deadbolt on the door and crushed it. The fragments littered the floor beneath him.

Hawke watched as Killian opened the cell door and walked inside.

Seemed that superhuman strength had come in handy yet again.

As Killian slowly moved closer to the boy, the look of fear and anger on his face was heartbreaking.

"Nikolai," Killian's voice was soft as he reached out his hand. "It's me, Mr. K."

Nikolai slowly focused on him. "Mr...K?" His tone was soft but raspy. The dryness of his throat matched his cracked lips.

"Yes," he stated. "It's me. We're here to take you home."

The sheer relief that rushed over him was obvious. He smiled and began to cry before he collapsed into Killian's arms.

"Just rest for now."

He brushed a small piece of crusty hair from the boy's face as he stood back up. Before he turned to leave, though, he looked at the two bodies that shared the cell with him. Those boys seemed to be about the same age and would never know what it was like to grow up, and though he wanted to try and save all those who were still alive, it seemed it was too late for them.

These thoughts caused his rage to grow as his heart ached.

As Killian came out, Hawke stretched out his arms and let out a small huff. It seemed most of his energy had come back. He wouldn't be running any marathons, but he could at least run now.

Which was a definite plus.

"Let's go," Killian stated.

"Agreed."

Luckily, it seemed like there weren't many workers in the hallways, so they were able to get to what looked like an exit in only a few minutes. They stopped at the edge of the hall and peeked around the corner. Two men in full military gear stood in front of a large ladder, which seemed to lead outside.

"Guess we'll need to find a different way to," Hawke was going to conclude, until he saw Killian set the young boy against a wall and make his way towards the guards. "What the hell?!," he loudly whispered as he tried to grab his shirt and missed.

The soldiers looked over and readied themselves as Killian approached.

"Who are you?" One of them asked.

"Seems like he's one of the subjects," the other stated. "We need to call in..."

CRACK!

The first soldier looked over. His partner's head faced him, but the rest of his body didn't

Fear rushed over him, but he had no time to react. Killian almost magically appeared in front of him and grabbed him by the side of his head with both hands. Tears streamed down his face as he was lifted from the floor.

Hawke watched in terror.

There was no remorse in Killian's eyes. In fact, it looked as if he was void of any emotion at all. An almost black haze covered his newly crimson shade before he pushed his hands together and...

CRUNCH!

The sound of flesh and bone being ripped and broken was all Hawke heard as he looked away. A second passed before he looked in time to see Killian drop the body and clean off his hands with the soldier's shirt. He said nothing as he walked back, picked up the boy, and made his way to the ladder. He reached for the first bar and, without looking back, said, "You coming?"

Hawke stood up and made his way over. "Yeah."

Killian went first and peeked out the small door at the top. It looked like an abandoned house, and for once, luck was in their favor because no one was there. It seemed like it was close to daybreak, so they needed to hurry and get out while it was still dark. Quickly but quietly, they climbed out, darted through the large side window, and made their way into the forest.

After they vanished amidst the trees, a camera shifted on the outside of the small house they had emerged from. Its feed was sent to a large room with multiple screens and computers set up all around.

"Dr. White," a young man spoke as he walked closer. "Would you like me to send soldiers to capture the subject?"

The doctor, clad in darkness, smiled and shook her head as she watched the camera feed. "No need. We can move into Phase 2."

The young man nodded and excused himself from the room.

As the doctor stood and crossed her arms, she watched the camera cycle again and stopped it just as Hawke and Killian entered the forest. A sinister smile curved her lips as she whispered to herself, "I wonder.... will the viper give in to his hunger and eat the hawk, or will the hawk slay the viper while his back is turned?"

9

Return to the Village

Sunrise broke through the canopy as Hawke and Killian weaved through the trees.

"God, this sucks!" Hawke yelled as he pushed through the pain and aches surging through his body with each stride. Although he had regained some of his strength, he was far from peak condition.

And it showed.

"We need to get to the village, but I have no idea where we are," Hawke stated as he glanced over.

When he did, however, he noticed something was off.

Killian was squinting as if the sun was blaring into his eyeballs.

"You good?" Hawke asked with concern for the kid. The last thing that boy deserved was being thrown to the ground because someone dropped him.

As Killian glanced over to Hawke, he realized it wasn't just his eyes adjusting to the daylight. His entire eyesight had changed. Everything was slightly out of focus, which irritated him immensely.

Of course, my eyesight had to change too.

He kept his thoughts to himself but did respond with a simple, "I'm fine, and I think I know where we are. Once we get a little further, I'll know for sure."

"What's a little further?" Hawke asked with a slight plea in his tone.

"There should be a large opening in the trees coming up soon," Killian responded as he darted around a tree. "It's the spot I use for landing when I need to make a quick stop in."

Silly me. Why wouldn't there be a landing area in the middle of nowhere?

Hawke didn't say it out loud, but oh, how he wanted to. "I hope you're right."

"Me too," Killian whispered under his breath.

Luckily for them, he had been.

They soon came to the clearing in the tree line, and there, in the center, was the landing pad. With no time to waste since he had their bearings, Killian took the lead and weaved back into the forest. Their bodies pushed through, running on adrenaline until they finally saw it.

Their goal was right in front of them.

Only seconds passed until Killian announced, "We made it," as they emerged from the forest into the center of the village.

Hawke leaned down, his hands resting on his knees as he tried to keep himself from falling over. He looked up through his gasps, but his eyes went wide.

A few villagers were putting handguns back into small holsters, either hidden underneath their shorts or their shirts. They had been waiting to see what came out.

Which was completely understandable given their trade.

Relief rushed over Killian as he smiled and collapsed to his knees.

One villager took Nikolai while another crouched down and put Killian's arm over his shoulder.

Exhaustion had finally caught up with him.

His body couldn't take any more.

He tried to fight it.

He needed to update the elder on what had happened and what their next step would be.

But that would have to wait till later.

His eyes shut softly, and he collapsed.

The villager adjusted his now limp body as another came out to grab the other side. They lifted him just as Clarice raced over.

She placed her hand on his cheek and smiled. "Rest now. You're safe," she said as she kissed his forehead and nodded to the village men. They nodded back as they headed towards the small house they were staying in.

THUMP!

Hawke fell to his knees as his legs finally gave out.

Two other men rushed over and grabbed him the same way they'd done to Killian.

"Thanks, " he muttered as they lifted him.

"You can rest too, Hawke," Clarice said as she looked over with a smile.

Hawke smirked as his eyes started to flutter.

"I'll...be...fine," he mumbled softly as his body shut down and passed out, too.

The next morning...

Small rays of sunlight flickered through the thin cloth curtains as Clarice walked through the door. She brought a small tray with two glasses of water and two small slices of bread. She placed the tray on the table between the beds before she leaned to the left towards Hawke.

"If you're going to fake being asleep, you'll have to do a better job than that, Hawke," she whispered in his ear.

Hawke smirked as he peeked at her. "You're good." He pushed himself up and stretched out his arms. "How long have we been out?"

"A day," she said as she handed him a drink. "Which is rather surprising considering how exhausted the two of you were." She then looked over to Killian.

After Hawke took his glass, she grabbed the other and stood next to the other bed.

"I'm glad you're doing alright, Mr. Blackwell," she stated as she extended her hand.

117

A smile and sigh escaped as Killian pushed himself up and took the glass. "Sometimes I think I've trained you *too* well, my dear."

She smiled softly before her face saddened and she clenched her hands together. "I was told to ask you if there were any other survivors besides Nikolai." Her eyes remained focused on the ground as she readied herself for the response.

Killian said nothing as he sighed and shook his head side to side.

Clarice's eyes glowed softly as she held back her tears, but she tried to keep her composure. She cleared her throat before she smiled and removed the plate of bread from the tray and set it down on the table. "I will leave you two to rest a bit longer," she said as she headed out. However, she stopped at the doorway and looked back. "The village elder wishes to speak with both of you after dinner this evening and,"

"Hey!" Hawke interjected. He clenched his fist as they made eye contact and he asked, "The boy...did he?" He knew this was not the best time to ask but he had to know if their effort had been in vain or if at least one good thing came from this.

A saddened but beautiful smile graced her face as she nodded.

"He's ok. One of the men took him to the hospital a little over an hour from here and we've been told he'll make it."

Hawke couldn't help but smile as relief washed over him.

"We'll be having dinner later so get some rest," she stated as she bowed and excused herself. The sound of the front door echoed through the home.

Hawke sighed in relief as he took a small sip from his water. He was just about to say something before he looked over and saw that Killian's expression had changed.

There, before him, was a broken man.

A man who had been turned into something destructive and chaotic.

A man who had once brought fear to all those who heard his name but now feared himself.

Hawke couldn't help but feel a small hint of sympathy for him.

Killian glanced over and quickly adjusted his composure. He snickered as he looked down at his glass. "Do you stare at everyone with such intensity, or is it just me?"

"Oh, don't flatter yourself," Hawke stated as he took a sip from his cup. "Even if I did play on that side of the rainbow, you would not be my first choice."

Killian laughed as he placed his cup down and moved to the edge of the bed. "Well, at least I know where I stand now." He stretched out his arms as he stood but stopped when he caught a glimpse of himself in the mirror across the room.

His attention drawn again to his hair and eyes.

He couldn't believe that terrifying thing in the mirror was him.

Of course, who could?

One small thing was in his favor, though. His eyesight was no longer out of focus. It seemed his body had just needed time to adjust to his new eyes.

Although Hawke wanted to say something to lighten the mood, he couldn't think of what to say. What *could* you say to someone who had been used as a lab rat and changed into something neither man nor beast?

Nothing. That's what.

"We'll figure out what they did to you," Hawke stated as he stood up and came to stand behind Killian, now looking eye to eye with him through the mirror. "And we will make them fix it."

"Either that," Killian muttered as he balled his fist. "Or I will make them pay with their lives for ruining mine."

BAM!

Pieces of glass rained down on the dirt floor as a small trickle of blood rolled down his wrist.

A short while later...

Hawke and Killian emerged from a house with their personal wares. Though they had been wearing the clothes from the lab, neither one of them wanted to keep those filthy things on.

So, they had done the only logical thing: turned on the furnace and burned them.

"We need to check around the village to make sure there aren't any spies watching us," Killian stated as they walked towards the forest.

"Agreed," Hawke responded as he rested his hands behind his head. He let out a small snicker as he said, "How about we not have a repeat of the last time, though?"

Killian smirked with his eyes forward as they broke the tree line. "Can't make any promises," he said with a hint of sarcasm.

"Aww man," Hawke jokingly whined. "I don't wanna get man-snatched again."

Killian stopped mid-step and looked over with his brow cocked.

"Man-snatched?" He asked in full disbelief.

"Well, yeah," Hawke responded as he stopped beside him. "We can't be kidnapped cause we're not kids, so man-snatched." The way he said it, like everyone already knew this fact, sent Killian over the edge.

He almost choked on his laughter and had to brace himself on the tree beside him. He had never heard something so ridiculous but also justified in his whole life. And, whether it be because of his transformation or the fact that Hawke said it, he just couldn't hold it in.

Hawke's expression went from confusion to slight embarrassment as he crossed his arms. "Ya don't have to laugh *that* much," he muttered.

Killian regained his composure as he wiped a tear from his eye. "Sorry, it's just..."

He paused.

A small smile broke through as he let out a sigh and continued into the forest.

"I can't even remember the last time I laughed like that," he said in a soft voice.

Hawke, again, looked confused but didn't say anything as he followed slightly behind.

As they walked, Hawke's mind started to think about what was going to happen to them after the mission was over.

Could he live his life like nothing happened?

Would Killian be able to go back after being turned into a monster?

If they couldn't cure him, would he be assigned to kill him instead?

Question after question ran through his mind until Killian said, "While we're here, I want to show you something."

Hawke reined in his thoughts as he saw Killian standing at the edge of the tree line. His thoughts had made him lose track of where they were, so he was very curious to see what it was. As they walked through, the sunlight blinded him for a moment, but as his eyes adjusted, he saw their new 'spawn point'.

It was a gorgeous lake.

The water was so pure that the sunlight and clouds reflected their image like a mirror. Small fish slowly swam to the bank before leisurely turning around and going back.

It was magnificent.

As Hawke gaped at the simplistic beauty, Killian reminisced about the times he had been here before. Images of children playing on the water bank as the adults smiled and relaxed in the sunlight calmed him. The villagers cherished this place and only shared it with those they considered one of their own.

"Beautiful, isn't it?" he asked as he glanced over.

Hawke smiled as he softly responded, "It is. Reminds me of where my grandma used to live. I'd go visit her during the summer when I was little. I'd always plead with her to let me go to the lake and swim and play with the fish. Obviously, being older, she couldn't let me..." He continued talking for a few good minutes about his Grandma.

Killian said nothing but smirked as he glanced back to the serene horizon.

He'd never known what having a grandparent was like. In fact, he didn't know what it was like to have parents either.

It's been a long time.

His thoughts paused as he looked back to Hawke, who was now going on about something concerning a frog.

He couldn't help but feel at ease around this guy.

And he had no idea why.

There was no reason they should get along. They should be trying to off each other every chance they had, but here they were.

Talking as if they had known each other a lifetime.

Like they were brothers.

And it was nice.

A stark contrast from the usual people Killian had around him.

He released a small sigh and walked towards the shore.

Hawke stopped talking.

He hadn't even realized he had been going like he was.

Thoughts of their situation ran through his head, but were cut off when Killian randomly stated, "I think we should take a dip in the lake while we're here," and without waiting for an argument or a smart remark, he pulled his shirt over his head and started removing his pants.

Hawke's eyes shot open before he turned away. "Dude! Could ya warn someone before ya start going all caveman natural!?"

Killian laughed as his pants and boxers hit the ground, and he made his way to wade waist-deep in the water. "Sorry. Thought you were more mature than an elementary school kid. I'll remember that going forward." His tone and smirk could be felt even without looking.

"Ya know what, prick?!" Hawke spun around with full intentions to lay into him but stopped.

As they locked eyes, Killian's hands gently caressed the water. His short silver hair glowed in the sunlight, and the definition of his body was god-like, but neither of those was what made Hawke stop.

What had made him stop was the dozens of scars painting Killian's body from his neck down to bottom of his back. They ranged in size, but one was more obvious than the others. It was very large, spanning from his right shoulder blade to his left hip.

And truthfully, it wasn't really the sight of the scars that left him speechless. Even being in his profession, he had a few himself.

No.

It was the sheer number of them.

Some had the angle and depth of a whip, while others looked like stabs from a blade. Some even seemed self-inflicted.

Killian broke the silence with a sigh.

Very people knew of his scars since he took extra care to cover them. Those who knew could be counted on one hand.

However, it wasn't that big of a deal that Hawke knew now.

He'd had already seen him turn into a blood-sucking monster. Not much lower you can go from that.

He turned his head and waded deeper. "There's a saying that goes monsters aren't born, they're made." He looked back from the corner of eye. "And I am no exception," he said before he dove in and vanished beneath the water.

Hawke stood at the edge and watched the small waves encase the rocks. Then looked out to the lake as Killian broke the water to come up for air. The rays from the midday sun made his skin and hair shine. He could almost be mistaken for a merman who would use his handsome features to lure unsuspecting women to their doom.

Shaking his head to banish those particular images from his mind, he looked out and groaned. "Maybe a bath wouldn't be so bad", he muttered. "Fine! You win," he stated loudly in defeat as he removed his clothes.

Once bare, he waded through the chilly water before he stopped waist-deep and looked around.

"Killian?"

He barely finished the name before something grabbed his leg and dragged him under.

He hurried back to the surface and gasped for air, but his ears burned with the cackling in front of him.

Killian stood with his hand on his hip as he laughed. "You might wanna watch where you step," he mocked.

Hawke wiped the water from his face and gritted his teeth before he leapt forward with the intent to bring Killian down with him.

It failed.

Killian moved to the right and enjoyed seeing Hawke face-plant the water. It made him laugh even more.

After he quickly recovered and looked back at his enemy, Hawke glared intensely. "Oh, it's personal now." He was about to continue their one-sided game of water tag before they both stopped and looked towards the forest.

RUSTLE!

Something was in the woods, and it was coming their way.

Instantly, they grabbed their clothing from the bank and dove underwater. They pushed through and went deeper to hide their shadows. Hawke was rather surprised, though. He was a good swimmer, but Killian was moving as if he really was a merman.

What the hell? What the fuck can't this guy do?

Unbeknownst to Hawke, Killian had been on the swim team in high school and college. Of course, that's information he'd learn a bit later.

A moment or so passed before they reached the other side. Killian was able to make out some overhang from the bank to which he pointed upwards and signaled Hawke for them to surface.

As quietly as possible, they both broke water. From their noses up was all they revealed as they looked back to the embankment. A few moments passed before two soldiers appeared and started snooping around. It looked like they noticed their footprints but assumed they had gone back into the forest. They said something to each other before turning and retracing their steps.

Letting out a sigh of relief, Hawke was the first to bring his head from the water. "That was close. A little too close for my comfort."

"You're not the only one," Killian said as he too came up. "Let's head out before they decide to check this side of the lake." He looked over and could see Hawke was already getting out.

He pulled himself from the water and stood dripping on the embankment.

Killian had to give the guy credit.

He had the body of a model. Truthfully, he was rather surprised. He knew from the file that Hawke was toned and took his strength seriously, but not to that level.

Hawke held up his now soaked clothing and muttered to himself as he rang out as much water as he could. He heard the splash of Killian getting out and the slow footsteps towards him. He thought nothing of it until he felt a soft breath against his neck.

Instinctively, he jerked around and jumped back. He dropped his clothes as he covered his neck and balled his fist. "What the hell is wrong with you!?" he loudly whispered. The last thing they needed was the bad guys finding them due to an irritated yell in the middle of the woods.

Killian stood with a smile, but it wasn't his usual shit-eating grin. It was more like a predator smiling before it ambushed its prey.

The hunger in his eyes was evident.

He wanted to eat.

Luckily, the loud whisper snapped him out of it. His eyes dulled a shade as he showed his irritation and scratched the back of his head as he gritted his teeth.

Hawke could tell Killian was... well...Killian again, so he dropped his fist and picked up his clothes. "I think you need to get your appetite under control before I have to do it for you....with my fist.", he said with a slightly smug expression as he slid his shirt on.

The comment made Killian smirk as he proceeded to ring out his own before putting them back on. "Well, in that case, I'll be sure to keep a tomato juice with me at all times after this." He walked past Hawke, who was still having a little trouble putting his pants back on, and said, "Wouldn't want you to hurt one of the good qualities I have."

"You have those?" Hawke retorted as he finished fighting with his clothes.

Killian sarcastically laughed as Hawke caught up with him and smiled at his own remark. They continued with their sarcastic whispered banter as they weaved through the trees and headed back to the village to warn every one of the unwanted company coming their way.

10

Loss of Appetite

Once they got back to the village, Killian headed towards the elder's home as Hawke went to their temporary base.

"Aren't ya going ta dry off first?" Hawke asked.

"I'm going to tell the elder about the soldiers we saw so he can get the village ready for an attack. I have a feeling it's coming soon."

Hawke had no time to argue before Killian was out of earshot. As he let out an irritated sigh, he got to the house and went inside. He made his way over to the table and began searching for one of the towels he packed.

After he rummaged through his belongings for a moment, he found his towel and pulled it free. He dried off his hair, set the towel on the edge of the couch, and then began to undress. He removed his shirt and then his pants and boxers, throwing them all on the floor. A sigh left his lips as he grabbed his towel once again.

"I don't know how much more of this I can take," he muttered as he dried off his chest and arms.

"Hawke," a soft voice spoke as the door opened around the corner.

Apparently, he had forgotten to lock it after he came in.

"I heard you were back and wanted to," Clarice stopped mid statement as she made eye contact with the fully naked Hawke in front of her. There was a very awkward second or two of silence before she turned around and darted back around the corner to the kitchen.

"I am so sorry!" she exclaimed from the other side. "I...I'll come back later!" She yelled as she darted out the front door.

Hawke, frozen for a moment by the shock of the situation, groaned and scratched the back of his head. "I can't seem to catch a break today." Though he continued to dry off, his head was racing as he tried to think of what he was going to say to Clarice the next time he saw her.

"Oh, hey," he sarcastically voiced out loud. "Sorry about ya having to see me butt-ass naked, but maybe ya should knock before ya come into someone's house next time." His less-than-serious smile faded into a rather unhappy frown before he threw the towel on the couch.

"What the hell do you say in a situation like this? I mean," he said as he reached into his bag and grabbed a change of clothes. "It's not like I haven't had a woman see me naked on plenty of occasions, but not by accident!"

Just as Hawke continued to banter while putting one leg into his boxers, Killian came through the door.

"Hey Hawke, why did I see Clarice…"

"Oh, for the love of fucking God, do you people ever knock!?" Hawke yelled as he fell over on the couch as his foot got caught inside his boxers from the shock of Killian coming in.

Killian said nothing as he went back and locked the door. When he got to the living room, he watched Hawke regain his composure and quickly put on the rest of his clothes.

A sigh left his lips as he started to remove his own damp clothes. "For future reference," he stated as he became stark naked on the other side of the table, facing his own bag, "there is an invention called a lock that you might want to use next time."

"There's something you might wanna blah, blah, blah," Hawke responded in a sarcastic and mocking tone. "I got it. Make sure the doors are locked next time I'm in my birthday suit."

"Yeah," Killian snickered. "Because I know I've definitely had my fill of the bird without feathers to last me a lifetime."

"Oh, shove it," Hawke mocked. "No one asked you."

"I know. I usually give opinions free of charge."

Killian finished getting ready before he turned to face Hawke. "Now that we're both dressed and dry, I'm going to head into the village. You rest for a bit. We need to be ready."

"Wait?" Hawke asked. "Whadya mean ready?"

Killian made his way to the door and looked back. "We're having guests for dinner tonight," he responded with a smile before he closed the door behind him.

"Guests? Dinner?" Hawke asked out loud. "I am so lost, but whatever. He said to rest, so I'm definitely gonna take him up on that. Don't know when I'll be able to catch some Zs again."

As he talked to himself, he made his way to the bedroom.

"Guess he'll fill me in later," he mumbled as he plopped down on his bed.

As his body relaxed and his head nuzzled into the pillow, a yawn escaped his lips. "Yeah. A nap will...be....", and as if on cue, his body found a spot and drifted off to sleep.

"Momma?"

A young Hawke ran through the darkness. Beads of sweat rolled down his face as they mixed with his tears. His torn white shirt and jean shorts were all he wore as his bare feet tapped against the dark floor.

"Uncle?"

No one answered him.

He stopped running, but it was a decision he instantly regretted. The floor vanished beneath him as he fell deeper and deeper into nothingness.

With a thud, his body came to a halt. He rubbed the back of his head before he clenched his hand that was resting on the ground and felt something hard. His eyes shot open as he looked down and saw skulls and bones all around him.

With all his strength, he tried to get up, but the bones seemed to come to life as they reached for him.

He screamed and cried, but no one came.

His voice gave out as the bones clawed at his shirt and skin until...

Water sloshed around him.

He swam as fast as he could to the surface. He broke the water as he gasped for air and looked around to see where he was.

There was nothing there.

Again, he was all alone.

Another tear rolled down his cheek before thunder echoed all around him. He turned, and to his horror, a massive tidal wave was coming.

Though it was futile, he tried to swim away as fast as he could.

The wave grew larger and larger as his body was swept up inside. The crash sent his body into a spiral. He didn't know which way was up or down. Before he could find his bearings, he found himself washed up on land.

He coughed up water as he shook to hold back his tears.

Soft voices broke through the bellowing sound of the sea.

He looked around and noticed a man and a woman walking away from him on the other side of the beach.

He quickly got up and darted towards them.

He got so close he could see who they were.

"Momma! Uncle!" he screamed as loud as he could. A smile finally broke his face as tears of happiness rolled down his cheeks.

Though he screamed, they didn't stop.

They continued walking like they didn't hear him at all.

He ran and ran until their distance closed as he grabbed both their arms from behind.

They turned their heads slowly, and the horror he saw caused him to trip as he backed away.

The woman's face was melted down into small pieces of muscle tissue and fragments wrapped around the single eye sitting alone in its socket. The man's face was no better.

His face was...nothing.

No eyes.

No mouth.

Nothing.

Just blank flesh.

He scrambled to his feet and ran. He didn't make it far before the depth of the sand caught his foot and made him fall.

"I want to go home!" he screamed through broken cries.

"Oh, but why?"

The voice echoed through the darkness as it swallowed him.

"You can't run from your past. You can't run from what you truly are," the deep, unknown voice taunted as it seemed to draw closer.

"What...," he stopped abruptly. He grabbed his throat as he tried to speak. His voice was gone. He couldn't even make a sound now.

"You know the truth," the voice whispered behind him. His head slowly turned. The darkness melted from the human-like figure in front of him.

It was him, covered in blood, with a smile on his face. "You know the truth," it taunted.

"You're just like him," it said slowly as it grabbed him by the neck. He gasped for air as he was pulled from the ground and dangled in the air.

"You know I'm right," it whispered as he pulled him closer and tightened its grip.

His vision started to blur, and his consciousness was fading, but not before the ghost whispered one more thing in his ear.

"He's not the only monster here."

Hawke shot up from the bed.

His breathing was ragged, and beads of sweat covered his body. His eyes darted around the room.

He was safe.

He wasn't in that horrible black abyss anymore.

He slowly tried to even out his breathing as he rested his head and arm on his knee. His other hand gripped the sheets tightly as his other leg fell to the side.

Not again...

It's been a long time since he'd dreamed a nightmare like that.

Years, in fact.

As he regained his composure, the front door opened to reveal Killian with two plates of food. "I brought food," he said as he set the plates down on the table. "Are you still," he started to ask as he came into the bedroom, "sleeping?" His question paused as he walked around the corner and saw Hawke's condition.

Killian knew that face.

Without making it a big deal, he turned and went back to the table. "I figured some food would help. We haven't eaten in days and need to strengthen up for tonight when the enemy attacks."

Hawke could tell Killian understood what happened.

This made the situation a little more manageable.

A sigh escaped as he stood and wiped away the sweat from his face. He then looked out the window and noticed that the sun was almost fully set. Apparently, he had taken a longer nap than originally intended.

Although he was a little irritated at himself for sleeping so long, Hawke changed his demeanor and snickered before he let out a relieving sigh and went into the living room.

"Ya don't have to be concerned about me. If we're going to be attacked, I'll be fine." He quickly struck an exaggerated strongman pose. "I mean, look at these babies."

Killian couldn't hold back a small laugh as he picked up his fork and watched Hawke take his seat. "Well, you keep those babies to yourself," he remarked as he grabbed a large bite from his plate and ate it.

SLAM!

Killian slammed his hand on the table as he vomited all over the floor beside him. His mouth dripped as he looked down at the mess beside him.

His face grew pale as he felt like another one was coming.

Instinctively, Hawke braced Killian's shoulders as he tried to stop dry heaving. He couldn't help but look over to the food and wonder if someone had poisoned it. Though he quickly purged that thought from his mind, given the relationship between him and the village.

After a moment, Killian signaled he was well enough to move and made his way, with some assistance from Hawke's shoulder, to the bedroom.

"What happened?" Hawke asked as he sat across from him on the other bed once Killian was lying down. Quickly realizing his statement was rather...obvious, he quickly corrected himself. "I mean, I saw what happened, but was the food just THAT bad?" He couldn't help but feel something was off.

"I don't know," Killian muttered between his small gasps. He had forgotten how much throwing up could take out of you, literally and figuratively. "The food smelled fine, but the minute it touched my tongue, it tasted like rotten milk mixed with aged tuna."

Hawke couldn't help but shiver at the rather grotesque description.

Although it was obvious something was wrong, Hawke couldn't help but feel it wasn't the food. He had the same meat and potatoes and he was right. They smelled delicious. Hawke took a moment to walk back to the table and grab Killian's plate.

As he came back in, Killian could tell Hawke was confused by what had happened.

Hell!

HE was confused about what happened.

He had eaten the village food every time he came here, and every time it was delicious and tasted of love and loyalty.

It was then that a thought crossed his mind.

A rather unpleasant one.

"You take a bite," he stated with a rather commanding tone.

Quickly looking over with a 'you're joking' expression, Hawke glanced down to the plate, then back to Killian. "What the hell do ya mean 'take a bite'?! I'm not touching that after what it did to you. Are ya trying to make me sick so you're not all alone in your suffering?"

Killian sighed but couldn't help smirk as he said, "As enjoyable as that would be, no, that is not the reason." A second passed before he sat up slowly and rested on the edge of the bed. His arms held him up as he looked over.

"Please..."

The level of fear behind his pleas shook Hawke to the bones.

He noticed his hands were shaking as he grasped the sheets. Killian had either figured it out or had a hunch about what had happened. And whichever one it was, it didn't seem like it would be a good thing.

After letting out a rather aggravated sigh and scratching the back of his head to help him think, he grabbed the fork from the plate and took a piece of the beef. He shoved it in his mouth and then...

Nothing.

Nothing happened.

In fact, the food was rather delicious. The meat was cooked perfectly, and the seasoning complemented the level of tenderness. Rather confused, Hawke swallowed and looked over.

The look of terror on Killian's face was gut-wrenching.

"Killian," Hawke said softly.

Killian's mind raced a mile a minute as his eyes darted side to side. He clenched his fists tightly and, without saying a word, stood up and ran out of the house. The slam from the door hitting the wall echoed.

"Killian!" Hawke yelled as he quickly set down the food and followed behind him.

When he made it outside, though, he was gone. The sun had fully set, and the only light sources were the torches set up around the village.

"Killian!"

No response.

"Damnit," he muttered as his eyes looked everywhere for a sign to which direction he had gone.

It was then that he saw Clarice running towards him from the other side of the village. "Hawke!" she yelled as she leaned over and rested her hands on her knees. "I just saw Mr. Blackwell running into the woods. What's going on?"

"Shit!" He yelled as he grabbed the torch from outside the house and darted towards the trees.

"I'll bring him back, don't worry!" Hawke yelled as he sped off.

Clarice watched as Hawke vanished into the darkness. The glow from his torch danced amongst the trunks as it grew smaller and smaller until it vanished completely.

11

Ambush

Subtle crunches and snaps echoed in the otherwise silent landscape as Killian ran and ran and ran until...

He broke through the tree line and gazed upon the lake.

The moonlight reflected off the water like a pristine mirror. The small sounds of wildlife accentuated the tune of the whistling breeze as it caressed the trees and bushes.

His small footsteps were barely audible as he made his way to the small dock. The water rippled as he walked and made the moon dance atop the lake.

He stopped just shy of the end and looked up. The full moon was like a midnight sun, which brightened his otherwise dismal eyes. A defeated sigh left his barely parted lips as he sat down, one foot swaying over the edge, as the other was pulled close and held up his arm.

"I can't do this," he whispered to himself.

Confusion.

Anger.

Sadness.

Emotions flooded his entire being as a small tear ran down his cheek. He wiped it away slowly.

He had lost everything.

His pride.

His composure.

His sanity.

All of it had been taken away.

He didn't know what to do.

His mind wandered as he gazed at the moon until he heard a small rustling behind him.

He quickly turned to see a small fire getting closer and closer. As well as a rather familiar voice calling his name.

He did nothing. He just turned around and continued his soulless gaze to the stars.

Hawke broke the trees and stared at the dark figure outlined by the night sky.

It was good he found him when he did. The fire on his torch was smoldering. Unfortunately, he had hit a snag on the way here and dropped one side into a small puddle. He was lucky it'd lasted that long.

As he set foot on the dock, he threw the torch into the lake. It quickly went out and softly vibrated the water.

When he got to the edge, he stopped beside Killian and looked down.

There he sat, motionless.

The shadows danced as if they were afraid to touch his toned physique. The radiance of the moonlight complemented his skin magnificently. It was as if one were looking at a painting.

Hawke sighed softly as he sat down beside him.

When he looked back over, however, he could really *see* Killian.

There was so much sadness and malice behind his eyes.

He could only imagine the disdain Killian had for those bastards at the lab. But what he knew hurt more was what he felt about himself.

The fact that he was no longer a man.

He had been transformed into the stuff of nightmares.

Hawke's eyes moved away as he looked up and joined in the silence. He had no idea what he was supposed to say. Of course, what could one say in a situation like this? It was something out of a horror novel, and those rarely ended well.

Before he had a chance to come up with something, Killian broke the silence.

"I don't think I can do this anymore, Hawke," he said, his voice cracking towards the last few words as his emotions tried to break through.

Hawke was shocked, but he kept his composure.

Killian was the one man he considered an equal on many levels, even though they had just met face-to-face a week ago.

"I can't eat human food," he said as he looked down from the sky and stared at his open hand backdropped by the lake.

"What do you mean you can't eat food?" Hawke asked, but deep down he knew what he meant. He just didn't want to say it out loud.

For the first time since he got there, Killian looked over. "Didn't you see what happened when I was at the house? You were there." His voice was low and filled with so much pain. "You had no problem eating it, so that means the problem is me."

Hawke looked ahead, breaking Killian's gaze.

"There's no way!" Hawke argued. "If that was true, then what are ya supposed to eat? Air!? It must have just been the food. Maybe your body didn't like it now, but when we leave and get back to the cities..."

"Hawke!" Killian yelled as he slammed his fist against the dock.

Hawke twitched as he looked over and saw his broken expression and the fractured wood beneath his fist.

"It wasn't the food, Hawke. I've had the villager's food countless times before, and every time it was delicious."

Killian paused as he let his other leg hang off the dock and stared at his open hands.

"I'm a monster now." His defeated tone sent shivers down Hawke's spine.

"No, you're not!" Hawke argued rather abruptly as he placed his hand on Killian's shoulder. "You are Killian Blackwell: Syndicate leader, fighter, leader, and a major pain in my ass," he smirked with the last descriptive words.

Killian put his hands down and let out a small laugh amidst his sigh. He could tell Hawke was trying, and that was more than enough.

"Never thought I would be getting cheered on by you," Killian said as he looked over, but his smile was quickly replaced by surprise.

Hawke's eyes were wide as what looked like a dart hit the side of his neck. Almost instantly, he collapsed forward into Killian's arms.

"Hawke!" Killian yelled as he shook him. His instincts were blaring as he looked back at the forest.

As he did, dozens of soldiers broke through and showed themselves.

I bet they followed the torch.

Killian's thought was spot on as the men's night vision goggles and guns shimmered while they slowly got closer to the dock entrance.

His blood began to boil as his eyes almost shown and dimmed simultaneously. A ripple of black melted into his pupils as he gently moved Hawke's unconscious body and stood up. With his fists clenched, he cracked his neck from one side to the other and licked the tip of his fangs as he smiled.

"I'm going to enjoy this," he whispered under his breath as the first wave of soldiers attacked.

12

Fight Between Allies

Killian darted forward with his fist pulled back. Within seconds, it met one of the unlucky soldiers' faces. The man flew back, knocking down the others like bowling pins.

Another raced towards him with a knife.

Killian grabbed him by the face, lifted him for a second, then slammed him into the ground. The sound of his neck breaking was heard over the thump of his body.

Two more attacked from behind, but they stood no chance against him.

He grabbed the blade from his previous foe as he swung his leg down and around, knocking them both off their feet.

Within the blink of an eye, he took the blade and stabbed one in the heart and the other between his eyes. Both lay lifeless as he adjusted his posture and turned to face the rest.

Blood oozed from the bodies around him, and as the waves hit the shoreline, their disgusting essence tainted the otherwise perfect water.

Killian watched as it disappeared into the vastness up to where Hawke still lay unconscious.

He needed to get rid of these pests quickly so he could focus on getting Hawke out of here.

With that goal in mind, he looked at the men with a fang-rearing grin.

"What? Are you waiting for an invitation?" He mocked as he majestically walked closer, which caused some of the soldiers to cower as they stepped back.

He looked through the crowd and grinned at the terror and panic that covered their faces. Some had even tried to hide their tears. He was relishing in their emotions, but there was one in particular who caught his interest.

In the back of the group was a rather tall man with broad stature. He stood with his arms crossed and wore a rather irritated gaze.

Must be the leader.

His suspicion was confirmed when the man bellowed out, "ATTACK", at the top of his lungs. The soldiers twitched and recoiled from the sudden scream, but quickly obeyed as some ran towards Killian, while others stood back with their guns armed.

Killian braised himself.

One soldier took the lead and came in with a machete. Killian dodged easily and tripped him, making him land on his face in the dirt.

Another pair leapt towards him, though they were quickly dealt with. He grabbed the neck of one and twisted with such force that his head faced the opposite direction. The other missed him completely and landed on the soldier who was still trying to get up from before.

It was then that the soldiers who stood back raised their guns to fire. Killian saw they had no intention to wait for their own men to get out of the way, which was a rather large advantage for him.

Gunshots rang through the trees as a barrage of bullets came for him. Armor-piercing rounds cut through the soldiers unlucky enough to be alive. Their screams melted into the sound of gunfire until they fell to the ground lifeless.

Killian's increased speed gave him another advantage as he outran their fire, if only by seconds or less.

As one of the men changed out his mag, he saw his chance.

He ran towards them, using the small window as his opening to attack.

Blood spewed from the soldier's neck as Killian ripped out his jugular. The other soldiers stood terrified for a second but quickly decided this was too much.

Most screamed and ran towards the woods.

"You're not going anywhere," Killian said maniacally as he dropped the flesh from his hand and raced to grab another man by the nape of his neck. He used his body weight to smash the man's head into the ground, killing him instantly.

The others continued to run, but it was to no avail.

He took down each of them, relishing in the feeling of adrenaline and the smell of blood.

Unbeknownst to Killian, however, the large soldier from earlier had used the chaos and mayhem to get to the dock.

He made his way to Hawke, who moved slightly as the drug started to wear off.

The soldier knelt next to him as the moon broke through a small cloud and covered him with a pale blue light. His muscles and definition were obvious even with his chest plate and other protective equipment. A name tag reflected against his chest.

Amos.

A sinister smile grew on his face as he began digging through one of the many pockets covering his pants. He then pulled out what seemed to be a small remote control.

"Owww." Hawke groaned as he blinked and rested his hand against his now pounding head. "What the hell?" He sat up slowly as he mumbled under his breath. He was still dazed from the tranquilizer, so he didn't notice his new friend right away, which was obvious to Amos.

With a small smirk, Amos leaned in and whispered, "You should have stayed unconscious."

The sound of the voice only inches away made Hawke's hair stand on end and his body stiffen. He slowly moved his hand and was terrified when their eyes met. There was so much evil behind those brown eyes, which accentuated his malevolent grin. The look sent a shiver down Hawke's spine, but his instincts took over, and he quickly tried to get away.

It didn't work.

His weak legs gave way beneath him, making him kneel on the dock. "What is," he said out loud, but quickly realized he wasn't completely over whatever had hit him earlier.

It was probably the same reason his head wouldn't stop pounding. His attention swayed long enough for Amos to make his way over and stand in front of him like a master before his slave. The pose alone made Hawke furious as he looked up and glared at Amos with hatred and contempt.

The malice behind his eyes made Amos flinch slightly as he took a step back. "I didn't think you had those kinds of eyes, little bird," Amos said as he looked down at the controller he had taken out before.

Hawke took notice of the device.

He wasn't sure what that little thing could be for, but he had a suspicion it wasn't anything good.

"Doesn't matter anymore, though," Amos said with a smile before he clicked one of the buttons.

"What do you," Hawke started, but was cut short by a horrible ringing in his ears and an unimaginable pain pulsating through his skull. He could not hold in his shrieks of agony as he grabbed the sides of his head and closed his eyes.

The ear-curdling screech caught Killian's attention.

He looked over just as Amos stood and walked away from Hawke.

"Hawke!" He yelled as he used a blade to slice a soldier's throat. He then pushed through the few remaining enemies and darted towards him. Luckily, the soldiers who were left could see they stood no chance against him and used the opportunity to escape into the forest.

Hawke couldn't hear him. In fact, he couldn't hear anything other than the horrendous ringing in his ears.

"Make....it......stop!" He screamed between clenched teeth as he collapsed against the dock, his head and knees supporting his bowing body.

The pain was so great that he couldn't take it anymore.

He leaned up slightly and banged his head against the wooden dock.

Again.

And again.

And again.

It wouldn't stop!

"AAHHHH!" Hawke released another nauseating scream as he leaned back to rest on his knees, the blood from the new wound on his head streaming down his face.

Killian reached the dock in seconds, but it had felt like an eternity.

His foot hit the dock, but when it did, something odd and concerning happened.

Hawke stopped.

His hands fell to his side as he just sat there, motionless.

Killian walked cautiously before he knelt beside him. He placed his hand on Hawke's shoulder and shook him. "Hawke?"

There was no response.

He leaned in close and looked into Hawke's still open eyes and was enraged. They were dulled and lifeless. It was as if his very soul had left him.

Gritting his teeth, he clenched his fist and looked towards the forest. The anger and rage boiling inside were hard to contain, but he knew where he was going to direct it.

"I'm going to kill him," he whispered.

He was about to stand and go after the bastard, but then he looked back at Hawke.

And was caught off guard.

Hawke had come to, but his eyes still showed no life behind them.

"Haw," Killian began, but was instantly cut off by a hand around his throat.

Slowly and methodically, Hawke stood up, dragging Killian up with him. The strength behind his grip was unnatural, and Killian knew his windpipe wouldn't last much longer.

With that in mind, he gathered his strength, and Spartan kicked Hawke's chest. Hawke stumbled back to the edge of the dock, and Killian jumped back to open more distance between them.

A few coughs broke the otherwise eerie silence as he regained his composure. He rubbed his neck softly and watched as Hawke looked at him. The pure contempt behind his lifeless eyes made him take a single step back. Before he had time to think, though, Hawke leapt forward to attack.

Killian dodged to the right but was taken aback by the quick recovery Hawke made. Without having time to react, he took a punch to the face and another to the gut. Spit sprayed from his mouth as what felt like a truck rammed into his stomach. As he stumbled back, his mind raced. He needed to knock Hawke unconscious so he could figure out what that bastard did to him.

But how?

He stood up straight as he readied himself for another attack. He looked at Hawke, who circled back towards the end of the dock, and it hit him.

That's how.

Before he second-guessed himself, he ran towards his comrade and collided with his midsection. They both went off the edge and…

SPLASH!

Chaotic ripples radiated through the water as they both went under.

He held on tightly while Hawke struggled to get free as they sank deeper and deeper into the watery abyss. Hawke joined his fists and brought them down on his back repeatedly, making it hard for him to keep his grip.

Unfortunately, no matter how strong someone was, hits like that would take their toll.

After taking another one, his grip loosened enough for Hawke to get a shot at his face and knock the air from his lungs. Before he swallowed too much water, he closed his mouth but lost his grip. It was then that Hawke used Killian's body and pushed himself towards the surface.

Oh no, you don't!

Swimming as hard and fast as he could, he caught up to Hawke and grabbed him by the ankle. Hawke then used his other leg and delivered a kick to his face. The kick released the grip and knocked him back.

Son of a!

His eyes glowed in anger as he watched Hawke swim towards the surface. He quickly caught up and grabbed him by the ankle again. This time, however, he grabbed both and pulled down as hard as he could.

Although there was resistance from the water, the force of his pull did what he had intended.

Hawke was now face-to-face with him.

He reared back his arm and...

BAM!

His punch made contact.

Hawke's head fell to the left but was quickly pushed back to the right as another punch landed. One after the other, punch after punch, Killian continued his onslaught relentlessly. Most were directed towards the head, but when Hawke started blocking, he moved his attack to the gut and ribcage.

He watched as bubbles slowly left Hawke's lips with each punch.

It won't be long now.

And he was right. With a final punch to the gut, Hawke let out his last bit of air.

Killian swam back a few inches as he looked on with a mixture of emotions.

Hawke wrapped his hands around his neck as he gasped, inhaling the lake water. His eyes rolled back in his head, and his arms fell to the side. Time stood still as his eyes finally closed and his body started to sink, showing he had completely lost consciousness.

The moment his body went limp, Killian swam and grabbed him by the collar of the shirt and made a break for the surface.

He grew closer and closer until…

SPLASH!

He erupted from the water.

He gasped for air, but there was no time to waste. As he wrapped his arm around Hawke's shoulders, he swam towards the shore.

As fast as he could, he dragged them from the lake. He pushed the corpses from earlier out of the way as he laid his comrade's now lifeless body on the ground with care.

He had to act fast.

He got on his knees and leaned Hawke's head back. Without a moment to waste, Killian leaned down, locked their lips together, and started CPR. After releasing a long breath, he leaned back up and began compressions. He repeated this step a few times, but nothing happened.

"C'mon, you asshole," he said between compressions.

With one final push, water rushed from Hawke's mouth as he gasped for air.

Killian turned him over and watched as water flooded from his mouth. He couldn't help but smile and let out a sigh of relief that he was alive.

The relief didn't last long, though. As soon as Hawke was able to breathe, he reached forward and grabbed Killian's shirt.

Killian didn't have time to react before he was put in a headlock and started gasping for air.

Damnit!

He screamed internally for foolishly dropping his guard. It was then, as his vision started to fade, that he saw his way out only inches away.

A taser.

Quickly, he grabbed it and flipped the switch as he stabbed the pins into Hawke's neck. The volts caused Hawke to seize and his grip loosen.

Killian gasped for air as he pushed himself from Hawke, who fell back on the ground. He then rubbed his neck and looked at his once again unconscious partner.

A few moments later, Hawke started to move again.

This time, Killian scooted away. He didn't want a repeat of that bear hug from earlier.

"Son of a," Hawke muttered under his breath as he pushed himself up and put his hand on his head. "What the hell?" He looked around and quickly saw the dead bodies. Seeing them made him jolt back to reality, but when he saw Killian, his nerves calmed.

"You know, you're a pain in the ass," Killian stated as he stood up.

Hawke huffed sarcastically as Killian knelt in front of him.

"I've heard that my whole life. What else is new?"

He rubbed his temple and a small headache lingered. Whatever they'd done had left him with one hell of a hangover.

"Do you have any idea what happcncd?"

"I don't," Killian answered quickly. "It looks like I wasn't the only one who got turned into a science project."

Hawke let out a small laugh which caused Killian to snicker.

It was good to see Hawke back to his normal self. They'd have to figure out the details of what happened later, though. Right now, they needed to get out of here and head back to the village.

"Well, let's," his words stopped short as shock covered his face.

Confusion washed over Hawke at the sudden stop in conversation but was replaced by horror when he looked up.

A machete protruded from Killian's chest.

His eyes looked past the blade to see the bastard who held it.

Amos.

With an evil smile, Amos kicked Killian forward. His body landed with a thud on Hawke's lap before the prick turned and made his way towards the forest.

"Have fun".

That was all he said before he sauntered off and vanished in the woods.

Hawke's anger boiled, and he wanted to chase after him, but he had more important things to worry about.

"Killian!" He yelled as he rolled him over to assess the damage.

Killian said nothing as his shirt-stained red. Small streams painted the side of his cheeks as he coughed from the puddle flowing up his throat.

He knew why Amos had stabbed him in the chest instead of cutting off his head.

But he wasn't sure Hawke had figured it out.

I have to tell him...

He looked up to Hawk, whose expression was easy to read. He had no idea what to do in this situation.

Hawke tried to think. Since the hit had been so precise, he didn't have time to repair the internal damage. He couldn't even open Killian's airway to help him breathe.

Killian raised his hand and grabbed Hawke by the scruff of his shirt. He coughed up another puddle of blood and before he could fill up again, he forcefully pulled him down to whisper in his ear.

"Run..."

His eyes shut as his grip relaxed, and his hand fell to the ground.

Hawke stared at the lifeless body in his lap. His mind raced with Killian's last words until he realized why he'd said that.

He took in a deep breath and regained his composure before he gently moved Killian's body from his lap and placed it on the ground.

He stood up and looked down at him.

The words had been a warning.

He knew he would come back.

It was why he'd told him to run.

He knew that he would come back starved for blood.

He knew he wouldn't be able to control his hunger.

An irritated sigh escaped as he scratched the back of his head.

I know I should leave, but...

He looked back at Killian.

The man just saved his life.

He'd saved him from whatever mind control those bastards at the lab had put in him.

What kind of man would he be if he left him like this.

Then a sinister thought bled into his mind.

You could just chop off his head and be done with it.

It only lasted a second.

He shook his head and released another sigh.

No! He saved me. I owe him, and debts are always paid.

He couldn't help but feel conflicted.

At the beginning, he would've been fine had Killian jumped from the plane or fallen down the stairs and broken his neck.

But now, he wanted to save him.

His mind raced until the small sound of rustling near the trees caught his attention.

He looked around until he figured out what was caused.

One of the soldiers from whatever the hell had happened earlier survived. He was trying to crawl to the woods with what appeared to be a broken leg.

Bingo.

His blue eyes dulled to the color of thunderstorms as he clenched his fists and made his way over to the crawling man. As he walked, he couldn't help but take in the carnage around him.

It didn't take long for him to slowly walk past the crawling man and stop a few feet in front. The man shook in terror and was drenched in a cold sweat. He trembled as he kept his head down and softly pleaded for his life.

The way the soldier acted reminded him of something.

But what was it?

Although the feeling of Déjà vu bothered him, he had no time to waste.

He squatted down and let out a small sigh. "Ya know ya brought this on yourself, right?" His tone was cold and monotonous.

"Please," the soldier pleaded, "please let me go." His voice shook as he failed to hold back his tears and they tapped on the ground beneath him.

"Please?" Hawke asked in a sarcastically surprised tone. "You ask me to spare your life when you were just trying to kill us. Now I ask," he paused as he reached forward and grabbed the soldier by his hair, pulling up to make the man look him in the eyes. "Does that logic make any sense? I don't think so." Malice oozed from him as he released the still pleading man's head from his grip.

He stood back up and looked down.

Disgusting.

He then walked behind him and, without a word, he knelt and grabbed him by his injured leg.

Rather forcibly, in fact.

The soldier let out a scream as the shock of pain and terror inside exploded.

Hawke paid it no mind.

He pulled the coward towards Killian's still body.

The man tried to plead with him as he struggled. He begged and screamed. The trees themselves could feel his fear.

But it was no use.

He let go of the man when they reached the entrance to the dock. As his victim writhed in pain, he methodically moved just a bit and knelt to a corpse that lay strewn beside them. He removed a hand knife from its sleeve and turned back.

He couldn't figure out why, but the feeling....

The feeling.... was intoxicating.

He stood back up with the blade in hand, tilting it to have the moonlight reflected from its sharpened edges.

His eyes shifted as he saw the soldier try to pull himself away yet again. Blood seeped from his wound as he scratched at the ground.

Hawke then examined the blade as he methodically walked towards him and asked, "Have you ever thought about death?"

The question caused the soldier to stop. He looked back as his cold sweat shone on his face and his lip quivered.

"It's a funny thing, actually," he continued. "Death is something all men fear, and it's the one thing that no man can conquer. It is the one guarantee we have in this fucked up world of ours."

As he spoke, he slowly circled the quivering man.

"But you know what makes it even more intriguing?" he asked as he knelt and placed the side of the blade against the man's face, slowly grazing his cheek.

His blue eyes glowed as the moon shone on his face.

But there was an aura around him now.

A terrifying one.

He leaned in closely and whispered, "It's when you take the fear of death and turn it into power."

Chills ran down the soldier's spine.

SLAM!

A blood-chilling scream echoed through the trees.

Hawke stood and stared at the blade now protruding from the man's back.

Blood slowly seeped into the fabric as his body convulsed and twitched as he went into shock.

And as Hawke stood there, watching him, a chilling realization hit him.

He didn't feel bad at all for what he'd just done.

In fact, he felt.....alive.

And that scared him.

He put his hand over his face as his breathing quickened. "What have I done?" He muttered as he tried to grasp what had just happened.

Although he had killed many men in his lifetime due to work, this felt different.

This time, he enjoyed it.

He'd never enjoyed it before.

He had killed countless people and though it didn't bother him, he didn't find any joy in carrying it out.

But this time…

He felt joy in every bit of it.

He took a step back.

Panic and fear swept over him as he tried to understand, but it was to no avail. He just couldn't understand.

RUSTLE

His head turned as he looked behind him.

The small sound he'd heard was Killian.

Or, at least, what *used to be* Killian.

The monster twitching on the ground was closer to a demon than a man.

Killian's eyes shot open as sweat rolled down his body, while his breathing was sporadic and terrifying. It was as if he were underwater, trying to take in any air he could. He shot upright but quickly fell back down on his side. His now elongated claws scraped the dirt beneath him as he balled his fists.

He looked up slowly to Hawke, who stood his ground and met his gaze.

Their eyes locked.

Killian couldn't help as saliva dripped from the corner of his mouth.

He wanted this to stop.

"Help....me," he strained between clenched teeth.

Hawke was surprised.

Killian seemed to have a better handle on his hunger than he gave himself credit for.

"I already have," he spoke with an almost malevolent tone as he pointed behind him at the soldier.

Killian's eyes widened.

He looked up to Hawke and smirked, allowing a small chuckle to escape between his clenched teeth.

He'd been wrong about Hawke.

He wasn't the goody-two-shoes he read about in his file. Neither was he an innocent bystander caught up in a nonredeemable situation.

No.

What he felt when he looked into his eyes was something he knew all too well himself.

Wrath.

In its true and unaltered form.

BA-THUMP!

Killian's body pulsated as the hunger inside him began to take control. He felt his sanity slipping as he balled his fists and blood seeped from his palms. He stared at the ground as a red hue began to cloud his vision. His mind raced while his body twitched and his breathing intensified.

Hawke, eerily unfazed by this, turned and walked towards the forest. He stopped beside the soldier but only long enough to kick his side and shock him awake. The man's breathing was mostly coughs as he looked around. He stopped, though, when his eyes saw Killian.

Fear took over, and he tried to scream. Small rasps and gasps were all he could muster from his strained and dry throat. "Plea....", he begged as he grabbed Hawke's pants.

THUD!

Hawke kicked the soldier in the face, which caused his body to roll over partially. The man tried to grab him again, but Hawke had stepped away. Instead, his attention moved to Killian, who had now mustered the energy to stand, although it was rather strained.

And when their eyes locked again, a shiver ran down his spine.

Those were the eyes of a predator.

A monster driven by hunger.

Killian crouched and crawled along the ground, his hands and feet methodically judging each step. As he did so, Hawke turned and made his way to the trees. With each step, he felt a little piece of his humanity die.

His back still to them, he waved his hand and said, "Bon Appétit."

The obvious smile on Killian's face would have been enough to scare the devil himself as his gaze moved from Hawke to the petrified soldier. His mouth watered as he imagined the taste of the blood pulsating in those veins.

The soldier's eyes met Killian's as he soiled himself. Urine and blood mixed as they puddled on the soil beside him.

Killian methodically inched his way closer until their faces were but mere inches apart. The soldier's eyes darted back and forth, but not for long. He blinked and Killian leaned down as he bit into the soldier's jugular.

Blood poured from his throat as Killian held down the man's forehead and his left arm. Although he tried to pull him off with his right hand, it was of no use.

Within seconds, the man's arm fell to the side.

Lifeless.

The hunger Killian felt was unlike any he had experienced before. The need for blood was screaming in his head.

More.

More.

MORE!

He leaned up, his teeth still clenched against the flesh, causing a rather unsavory sound to echo through the forest. The flesh mixed with blood was something he could not describe.

Pure bliss consumed him as they came together in his mouth. The consistency and texture rippled through his senses as shivers ran down his spine.

MORE!

His mind raced as desire rushed through his body. With each grind of his teeth, he grew hotter and hotter until he swallowed, and it sent waves of euphoria through every nerve. He leaned his head back and released a siren's scream as tears rushed down his rose-colored cheeks.

He looked at the desecrated body and smiled.

Not another thought crossed his mind as he leaned back down and feasted on the rest of the blood and flesh the man had to offer.

Bite after bite.

Piece after piece.

His euphoria grew and grew till nothing of the man was left.

Only the monster remained.

Unbeknownst to him, Hawke had stopped at the break in the trees and watched. His face was clad in horror, but an uncharacteristic smirk rested on his lips.

Hawke couldn't help it.

For some reason, the sight of Killian giving in to his hunger in front of the radiating moon and clear skies was...

Beautiful.

He shook his head and released an aggravated sigh before he continued. His mind raced as images of the man he sacrificed flooded him.

A few steps later, he stopped.

His eyes grew wide as he clenched his fist.

He remembered.

He remembered why the soldier's face seemed familiar.

It was the same look he'd worn when Killian bit him at the lab.

The undeniable expression of pure fear.

Another sigh escaped as he continued towards the village. He placed his hands in his pockets, and as he sobered his mind and maneuvered through the trees, he broke the otherwise deafening silence around him with a gentle statement.

"Guess we're both monsters after all."

13

Attack on the Village

Darkness enveloped Hawke as he methodically made his way through the trees and brush. The deafening silence was broken only by his somber footsteps.

He walked and walked until he saw the flickering dances of reds and oranges painting the black and blue of the night sky.

"Guess I gotta tell the elder what happened," he whispered as he continued.

However, once he broke through the trees, it didn't take long for one of the villagers to notice him. They yelled, drawing everyone's attention.

"Hawke!" Clarice exclaimed as she rushed towards him, followed closely by the other children.

"We were so worried about you both, and wondered," her voice trailed off as she looked past him, examining the woods. "Where is Mr. Blackwell?"

Hawke looked down.

Clarice covered her mouth as she shook her head.

"He's alive," he said as his fist tightened. "He's just tied up at the moment."

The relief that swept over her and the other children was priceless.

It was obvious how much he meant to them.

Which made the next conversation he was going to have that much harder.

He had to explain to the elder how their proverbial knight in shining armor had turned into a flesh-eating monster from a 90's horror movie.

The elder made his way through the crowd and stopped before Hawke, allowing Clarice to gather the children and excuse themselves.

"Sir," Hawke's voice was cold, but a small hint of sadness was there, too. It was never easy to deliver bad news, but this one was a doozy.

The elder raised his hand to quiet him. "You said Killian was still alive, correct?" His tone was stern.

A small sigh escaped as Hawke nodded.

"That is all I need to know," the elder responded.

"But," Hawke tried to interject.

"But nothing, Mr. Hawke." The no-nonsense tone of the elder's statement took Hawke by surprise. "Regardless of what Mr. Blackwell has done," there was a small pause, "most of us would not be alive if not for him."

He gingerly smiled as he sauntered closer to Hawke and signaled for him to lean in so he could whisper. "No matter what monster he's become, he's still our savior."

Hawke's eyes widened as he turned and looked the elder in the eyes.

How did he know?

"How do you..."

The elder raised his hand once more, but this time his interjection was followed by a smile. "You can't hide anything from the elderly. Haven't you seen enough movies to know that?"

Hawke snickered as he smiled.

And then, as if the universe itself decided to ruin their small but beautiful moment...

BAM!

A loud explosion reverberated from the edge of the village.

Fire rolled against the depth of the night sky as the elder and Hawke stood in horror. Hawke darted towards the fire, pushing through the chaos of the running villagers.

Just as he reached it…

Three large Jeeps emerged from the forest and barreled through the village. Gunshots rang out as the villagers screamed.

Hawke turned and raced towards the house to grab a weapon, narrowly dodging two of the Jeeps as they drove past him.

He rammed through the door and grabbed his MP5 from the bag.

As if a well-oiled machine, he grabbed his extra clips and attached one to the gun itself. Once loaded, he ran back out and surveyed the damage.

What he saw when he came out was definitely not what he had expected.

Most of the women and children were gone, and the men were now holding AKs and other automatic guns, firing back at the enemy.

What the hell is up with this village?

He would definitely need to have a sit-down with Killian once this was all over.

He had a feeling he was missing something.

However, he had no time to dwell on it.

One of the Jeeps drove by and released a Molotov Cocktail on the house beside him. Instinctually, he aimed his gun and...

BANG!

He nailed the one who threw the bomb in the back of the head and watched as his body fell and hit the ground.

Gunshots rang from one side to the other as two more Jeeps came from the woods. These, however, stopped to block the road as a dozen soldiers joined the fight.

Hawke darted behind one of the buildings as he surveyed the new enemies.

His eyes widened, then narrowed in rage as one soldier in particular caught his attention.

Amos.

His blood boiled for revenge against that son of a bitch, but he needed to rein himself in. It would be pointless for him to charge in headfirst and wind up dead.

He wanted nothing more than to stand over Amos with his gun planted firmly to his temple and...

"Calm down, Hawke," he muttered under his breath between clenched teeth. "You'll have your chance."

He took in a few deep breaths to clear his mind.

As he did, he emerged from behind the house and started shooting at the soldiers. His aim was impeccable as they fell.

One by one.

Bullet for bullet.

He replaced his clips one after the other with no pause between his movements. Though he was taking them down, it wasn't enough.

He wasn't making enough headway, even with the villagers helping.

The soldiers soon took shelter, and the large automatic guns attached to the back of the Jeeps kept them at a distance. "Damnit!" He yelled as he ducked behind one of the houses. "Where the hell is a diversion when you need one?"

BOOM!

One of the enemy's vehicles at the end of the road exploded.

"What the hell?" Hawke quickly looked around the corner and saw the last thing he expected.

It was Killian.

The flames radiated behind him as he threw the dead soldier to the ground. The benevolence in his crimson eyes matched the rage of the fire. His tattered clothes and blood-stained skin made him the stuff of nightmares.

Which suited him perfectly.

The enemy turned their attention and opened a barrage of fire.

Killian paused, but for only a moment, before he ran through the men, ending most of them quickly.

Blood spewed from their wounds, which ranged from gashes on their chest to slits on their necks, but all five who had fired were dead.

Hawke stood in disbelief.

He knew Killian had become stronger, but what he saw was unbelievable.

What the hell is he?

His mind raced as he realized his increase in speed and strength probably had something to do with his last meal.

The images of the soldier flashed through his mind, but instead of sadness or concern, he felt...

Satisfaction.

In fact, a smirk broke his lips as he thought about it.

I wonder what's left of that poor soul's body now.

His eyes widened as he shook his head and sighed.

What the hell is wrong with me?

Thoughts like that had never crossed his mind before.

Especially to the point that concern and sadness were replaced by contentment and pride.

I need ta see a shrink when I get back.

A scream broke his spiral as another soldier fell to Killian.

This time, he stood with part of the man's flesh hanging from his mouth. He lifted his head slightly and slurped it down. His eyes then darted from one enemy to another until they settled on one in particular when their eyes met.

"Amos", he growled between his clenched fangs.

As Killian readied himself to attack, Hawke raised his gun and lined up a shot at Amos.

Right between his eyes.

Amos had stood watching as his men were slaughtered one by one.

His demeanor had not changed at all.

That is, until he made eye contact with Killian.

Even Hawke could see the shiver go down his spine.

It made him smile.

It was short-lived, however.

Looking over a split second before Hawke fired, Amos dodged the bullet and took cover behind one of the Jeeps.

Killian snarled and darted towards him but was met by an unexpected roadblock.

The Jeep Amos had darted behind flew through the air towards him, forcing him to duck an instant before it hit. It slid and came to a stop down the roadway as Killian stood back up.

When he turned, his eyes widened in unison with Hawke's as he slowly relaxed his gun.

Well, what *used to be* Amos.

It seemed the crazy bastard had injected himself with something.

He stood over 8 feet tall, muscles bulging from his arms and legs, as a black, blood-like fluid surrounded sporadic parts of his body.

"HAHA!" Amos roared in laughter, which echoed through the village. Everyone, including his own soldiers, stopped and stared.

"Now you will die!" He yelled as he ran towards Killian and reared back his fist.

Killian barely dodged as he jumped to the left. The impact shook the ground and created a small crater beneath Amos's hand.

Killian landed a few feet over and stared as his mind paused its hunger.

It realized this man was a threat and needed to be dealt with in a very particular way.

He yelled as he jumped from the side of the house he had landed on and reared back his own claws to attack. They made contact as he swiftly dodged another hit and ran past him. Killian slid as he turned to see how much damage he had caused.

The monster snickered slightly as Killian's eyes grew wide.

The wound boiled with black liquid before it healed. It looked like there had never been a wound there to begin with.

"Awww c'mon!" Hawke yelled as he ran towards Killian, kneeling next to him.

The two looked at each other before Hawke asked, "You still in there, Killian?"

The tone of his voice was a mix of concern with a slight hint of fear. Although he would never admit it, Killian absolutely scared the shit out of him right now.

Killian understood but could not answer. It took every ounce of his control to resist the urge to devour him. Not because he wanted to, but the pure urge of hunger he felt was hard to control at the moment.

He was able to nod, though.

Which was more than enough for Hawke.

"Good," Hawke said as he looked back at Amos. "You distract him while I try something out."

The vagueness of Hawke's plan had Killian rather concerned, but it was all they had. He nodded, then jumped forward and engaged with Amos again.

Before he ran off to tackle his side of the plan, Hawke couldn't help but stare as the two monsters attacked each other. He ticked his jaw as he turned and darted towards the two Jeeps at the end of the village.

I'm glad one of those is on my side.

He focused on his goal as another thought instantly came after his last one.

At least, for now anyway.

Lucky for him, the Jeeps weren't too far off, and almost instantly, he had his eyes on the prize. A smirk broke his lips as he reached down and picked up a rocket launcher.

"Bingo."

He loaded the barrel quickly and turned to the fight in time to see Killian thrown towards one of the houses, demolishing it in the process.

Killian stood slowly as he pushed the debris away.

His wounds varied from superficial to gashes in which bone could be seen.

The wounds quickly healed themselves as his own blood gargled and melted to cover them.

But the pain he felt was anything but quick to dissipate.

It also didn't help that the more blood he lost, the more intense his hunger became. He had to finish this soon, or any sense of self he had left would be gone.

He darted forward and leapt high into the air, landing on Amos's back.

Amos struggled to reach him, but his bulky arms wouldn't allow it.

Killian saw this as his opportunity and slashed at the back of his neck; each one taking flesh and spraying blood all around him.

Amos screamed in agony, but his healing abilities were a step ahead of Killian. As fast as Killian carved, his flesh healed back. Hawke, trying to line up the best shot, saw this as his opportunity.

"Killian!" He yelled. "Get out of the way!"

WHOOSH!

The rocket left its chamber and streamed through the air.

Killian watched as the missile grew closer and closer, but, as if time had slowed down, he realized that if he stopped distracting Amos, he would have a chance to dodge. His eyes softened for a split second as he looked back at Hawke.

It was then that he made his choice.

"KILLIAN!" Hawke yelled at the top of his lungs. His eyes widened as he saw the look in Killian's eyes as the rocket made contact.

BOOM!

A cloud formed as a weary silence fell upon the once rampant battlefield.

It seemed the villagers had taken care of the other soldiers, who were all either dead or tied up. The smoke cleared slowly as Hawke dropped the launcher and ran.

"Killian!" He yelled.

"Killian! You son of a bitch!" He continued as he looked feverishly through the smoke.

"Where the hell...are...you.." His voice trailed to almost a whisper as he stopped inches from one of the bodies.

Killian's body.

His back was scorched, and his shirt was completely gone.

The scars from the battle didn't heal like they had before. In fact, blood slowly seeped from his wounds and saturated the ground around him.

Hawke fell to his knees as he stared at the horrific scene.

"Aggghh," a hoarse voice was heard from behind.

Hawke's eyes widened as he looked back and muttered, "There's no way."

Unfortunately, it seemed there was.

Amos pulled his body along the ground towards him. Pieces of flesh and the black ooze melted from his bones as he said with a raspy voice, "You will...not...defeat me."

The squishing sound of his body decomposing caused Hawke to look on with disgust. He grew closer as nothing but his upper body remained.

"I...will...win," he mumbled as his voice softened to a whisper and he collapsed on the ground.

His hand was inches from Hawke as it slowly melted and joined the disgusting pile of flesh and bone.

The ooze drifted in all directions, some almost touching him until he moved out of the way. However, when he stood up and moved in front of Killian, he was able to get a better look.

"Oh, Killian," Hawke whispered.

It was worse than he thought. His face was unrecognizable due to third-degree burns that continued down his right side. Reluctantly, he knelt and slowly shifted the body.

What he saw would make even the strongest man look away.

The other side of his face was almost completely undamaged, but the horrific wound to his chest was nauseating. His heart was mangled while his veins and muscles cupped its pieces.

Unbeknownst to anyone, Killian's blood slowly gathered and moved through the debris. The small trail almost danced between rocks and dirt until it met with a small puddle of the black fluid that was once Amos.

Like a malicious serpent, the fluid slithered up the blood trail and seemed to devour it.

It wasn't until it crept over Killian's shoulder that Hawke jumped back.

"What the fuck?"

The slow, methodical way the oily substance covered his body was mesmerizing. It was like a blanket covering every inch of him. It moved from his arm to his side, then to his legs, and finally to his neck.

Hawke couldn't bring himself to do anything but watch. He was terrified that he would be consumed if he touched it.

He couldn't help him.

As the seconds passed, he thought it was over when all but Killian's head had been covered and the sludge stopped moving.

But it wasn't.

Killian's body slowly melted into the puddle that surrounded him. It was as if the land itself was swallowing him whole.

"Killian!" Hawke yelled as he reached out to grab him.

But he hesitated.

Which was all it took for the darkness to swallow the rest of him.

Deafening silence echoed for what felt like forever.

The smudge didn't move again. It bubbled slowly as a scream broke the silence. One of the women cried and fell to her knees while others could do nothing but stare at the puddle.

The utter disbelief and terror on his face were indescribable. He had never seen anything like that before.

In fact, he wished he could unsee it. His eyes darted back and forth on the ground as panic started to set in.

What was he gonna do now?

Killian was gone, but he had to finish the mission.

How would he do that without him?

Where did he go?

What happened to his body?

Question upon question sent his mind spiraling.

He couldn't focus.

Nothing was making sense anymore.

"What the hell is going on?!" He yelled as he punched the ground. He then reigned in his thoughts and got up with a sigh. Sitting on the ground wasn't going to help anyone. He had to think of what to do next.

He turned to speak with one of the villagers but was met with looks of rekindled horror and confusion. He could tell they weren't looking at him, but what were they…

No…

He slowly looked behind him.

His eyes widened as he stared at the puddle.

But it wasn't only the ooze there anymore.

A malformed arm slowly rose from the abyss and grabbed at the soil beside it.

Hawke couldn't believe what he was seeing.

Though he was shocked, his mind was clear enough to know that whatever that thing was, there was a chance it would be their enemy. He turned and yelled to the villagers, "Get back! Get everyone inside!"

The men quickly directed everyone away as the dark liquid pushed itself up and slowly formed the shape of a human.

It crawled from the pit as if coming from Hell itself.

Carefully, it slowly pulled its body against the ground, and as it cleared the goop, it collapsed a few feet from him.

The puddle then seeped into the earth below, leaving the black figure alone.

Hawke took a moment to calm himself.

He didn't know what to do.

Apparently, they had removed *Monsters and Other Miscellaneous Beings* from his training syllabus before he joined the CIA, so he was at a loss.

He breathed slowly as he leaned down closer to whatever *it* was.

As he did, bubbles began to pop along its back.

He recoiled.

The sludge moved and revealed skin as it melted away.

The soft, colored contrast of skin poked through as it vanished. It seeped into the ground just like before, and all that remained was a man.

But not just *any* man.

"Killian?" He softly questioned.

It was him.

Well, it looked like him anyway.

There were no wounds from the battle earlier, and in fact, at all.

The scars that once riddled his back were gone.

Its hand twitched.

Hawke stepped back.

Slowly, it moved and pushed itself up. As it stood, it rubbed its temple and blinked.

"Son of a...", it muttered.

The thing even sounded like Killian.

"Killian?"

It blinked a few times as it looked over.

"Hawke?"

The confusion in its words made Hawke flinch. It was then that it made eye contact with him.

When their eyes met, Hawke knew within seconds.

That thing that came from the ooze was Killian.

No doubt about it.

"Killian," Hawke stated as he walked closer. "What the hell happened to ya?"

"I...don't know," Killian responded as he looked around. "I remember fighting Amos and then you shot...the..." His voice trailed off as he looked at his hands and chest. He slowly felt his back, and confusion came again when he couldn't feel his scars.

He also noticed he was naked, which was rather embarrassing.

Slowly, he leaned down and grabbed a piece of black fabric that most likely had belonged to his shirt. He wrapped it around his waist, but all the while, his eyes seemed distant.

"What.... happened to me?" He asked softly.

"That's what I'd like to know," Hawke responded as he closed in and placed a hand on his shoulder. "Your face and body were destroyed," he stated. "There's no way you should be alive right now."

Killian sighed as he responded. "I know."

BA-THUMP!

He winced violently.

Hawke jumped back.

"Nooo," Killian pleaded as he fell to his knees.

BA-THUMP!

"AGGGHHHH!" He screamed as he grabbed his head and slammed it to the ground.

Hawke stood back as panic set in.

He knew what was happening.

He had to get Killian under control, or he'd lose it.

If that happened…

We're all gonna die.

He didn't have time to think.

He had to do something.

He jumped and grabbed Killian in a full nelson. Though he had him constrained, it wasn't by much and wouldn't last long with Killian's strength growing by the second.

"I need help!" Hawke yelled.

Without hesitation, five of the village men ran and joined him. They grabbed his legs and two took Hawke's spot as he got out of the way.

Killian's screams turned into growls as he threw his arms and tried to break free. In the chaos, one man was thrown towards the debris as another smacked the side of a building.

The men were alright, luckily, and after a moment, they had him subdued.

Barely though.

Hawke stared at the beast and wasn't sure what to do next. He was running on pure adrenaline now and wasn't in the right state of mind to come up with a plan.

"Cover him up and take him to the bunker!" The elder yelled as he came to stand beside him.

"The bunker?" Hawke questioned. Although he had not seen the whole town, a bunker was not something he thought would be there.

"Mr. Blackwell had us build a bunker in case a situation arose. Being part of the Syndicate is a dangerous job after all." The elder stated as he watched the villagers struggle to carry the beast away.

"Guy has a plan for everything, huh?" Hawke's almost silent voice vanished amidst the noise Killian made. His heart ached for him.

Wait? What the hell?

Hawke stood silent as his eyes followed.

It has been ages since his heart hurt this much for someone, but how could it not?

The man who had gained his respect, in some weird and twisted way, was gone.

What was left was something completely different.

He was a monster.

But he...

He was also...a victim.

Thoughts raced as the men opened the bunker and took Killian inside. Since he was still weakened from earlier, he was unable to run as they came out and locked it.

He was now a monster in a cage.

"Mr. Hawke?"

The elder's voice snapped him back.

"Yes, elder?" His eyes were still focused on the door.

"Do you know what's happened to Mr. Blackwell?" He asked as he too was focused on the bunker.

"I do," he stated.

"I see," the elder responded.

"Ugh," Hawke groaned as his head started to spin. The adrenaline and anxiety he'd felt vanished as he calmed down, and now exhaustion took over. He stumbled back but caught himself before he fell. He collapsed to his knees, then to the side.

The elder and other villagers raced to him; their voices all jumbled together incoherently.

He was fading fast.

He needed to tell them what to do.

They had to know what Killian needed.

He reached out to the elder.

"He…needs…to feed," his words barely a whisper as he fell unconscious.

14

Clad in Armor

Blinding darkness surrounded Hawke as he looked around.

His eyes searched for any sign of light, but to no avail.

It was as if his sight had been taken completely.

Fear took root as he started to panic.

He released a scream, but...

There was no sound.

He tried again, but nothing.

The silence was deafening.

He could hear his blood as it pumped through his veins.

His breaths were ragged and loud as he tried to calm down, but it was no use.

His anger festered, and he couldn't hold it in.

He screamed, "Are you going to take everything from me!?"

His voice echoed through the once-silent depths.

He could speak again.

Relief washed over him, but only for a second before...

"I will take it all away," an eerily soft voice responded.

His hair stood on end as chills ran over him. He looked around and tried to find where the voice had come from.

Unfortunately, it didn't take him long.

As if appearing from the abyss itself, there, only inches from his face, was himself.

Though this version was different.

He stood covered in blood and wore a sinister smile. His eyes glowed an almost sun-like yellow as they stared into him.

"Why?" He asked, but his form had changed. He was now a child, sacred and powerless. Tears gathered in his eyes as he looked to the ground.

"You don't deserve happiness," the man taunted.

He sauntered around him.

"You are worthless."

"You are nothing but a murderer."

"A man who deserves to die."

As the shadow spoke, Hawke's body fluctuated between his adult and child form, but his head never raised. He continued to stare at the ground in shame.

"Maybe I do," he muttered as his adult body collapsed to its knees.

He looked at his hands as his doppelganger stopped behind him.

"You do," the blood-chilling voice responded as it placed its hands on Hawke's shoulders. "Just give in and let your soul succumb to the depth of your sorrow."

Memories flooded him.

His mother was a beautiful woman, but all he could see was her cold body in its casket, holding the small bouquet he had picked for her.

An agent he'd served with screamed during an ambush before he took a bullet to the head.

A child involved in a suicide bombing cried in his arms before she took her last breath, and blood soaked his hands.

And then there was Killian…

As his mind raced, the being behind him slowly turned to darkness and began to consume him. The black hue covered his back and wrapped around his body like a cold embrace.

His eyes glazed over as his mind thought about his adversary. Although they were enemies, he viewed him as a brother.

In fact, he had secretly felt jealous.

The man had everything, including a kind soul.

One that saved those the world ignored or threw away.

He had wanted to tell him how he had grown to respect him.

But now he would never have the chance.

"What do you mean you'll never have the chance?" A somewhat familiar voice said.

Hawke snapped back to his senses, which caused the darkness to retreat.

"Killian?" He questioned as he stood back up. "Where are you?"

"I'm right here."

He turned quickly as Killian appeared.

They stood eye to eye as Hawke noticed he was in his usual garb of a suit and tie.

"You can't give up now," he said as he placed his hand on Hawke's shoulder. "We have to get out of here so I can kick your ass." He snickered softly as he nodded.

Hawke was taken aback but couldn't help but feel relieved.

"Out of everyone who could've helped snap me out of this, it had to be you, huh?" He smiled as he placed his opposite hand on Killian's shoulder. "And don't think it will be that easy, asshole."

"Good. In that case..." Killian responded, then leaned in with a whisper.

"...it's time to wake up."

"Uggg," Hawke groaned as he slowly came to.

He blinked a few times to regain his composure and saw it was still nighttime.

"Thank god," he stated as he pushed himself up. This meant it hadn't been long since he passed out.

A hand touched his back, causing him to twitch and rear back his fist.

It was one of the villagers.

He put down his arm and let out a small sigh.

"I'm glad you're awake," the elder said as he came around to stand in front of him.

"How long was I out for?"

"Not long," he responded as Hawke slowly stood up. "About ten minutes."

To him, it had felt like an eternity, but that was one obvious downside to nightmares.

Time had no meaning to them.

A second or so passed before Hawke looked to the elder with saddened eyes. "Is Killian?"

The elder shook his head.

"Damnit!" Hawke shouted as he scratched the back of his head.

"Mr. Hawke," the elder looked up to him. "You mentioned before that Mr. Blackwell *needed to feed*. What exactly did you mean by that?"

Hawke's eyes shot open, but he quickly regained his composure. "That's a bit difficult to explain."

"Please," the elder pleaded as he placed one of his hands on Hawke's shoulder. "We deserve to know."

Hawke didn't want to tell them. He didn't want to tell them that the man they all looked up to was now a ravenous monster that might eventually eat them. He really didn't want to, but...maybe the dedication they felt would give them reason enough to help him.

"Ok," Hawke reluctantly stated. "I'll tell ya."

Several minutes later...

"And that's where we're at now," Hawke stated as he finished telling the elder and villagers who had gathered around Killian's current situation.

Some of the women were crying on behalf of his suffering, while the men clenched their fists in rage. The elder's hands shook on his cane as he looked to the bunker where the sounds of the hungry beast inside had died down. "So you're saying he needs to drink human blood to regain his senses," the elder stated.

Hawke nodded, but as he did, he caught a glimpse of the unconscious prisoners the villagers had captured from the raid. His head turned as his eyes grew wide before narrowing into a stare.

His demeanor changed.

Just like earlier in the forest.

"We could use them," he stated with ice-cold words.

The elder looked at the prisoners, then back at Hawke, and finally at them again.

"You're right," he stated. "We can." The quick agreement from the elder caused Hawke to cock his brow, but he would open that can of worms later.

Right now, he had to get Killian under control.

"I need three of you to help me carry them," Hawke stated as he made his way over to the four prisoners. Almost instantly, three of the village men volunteered and grabbed the other three.

They made their way over and stopped in front of the barracks.

The large metal doors sat slightly inclined off the ground, appearing like nothing more than a basement. Hawke realized their normality was the reason he hadn't noticed it before.

"Open the barracks," Hawke subtly commanded.

The elder nodded to two of the other men, who then proceeded to unlock the doors.

"Once I clear the stairs, bring the other men down and leave them," Hawke ordered as he carried a soldier over his shoulder through the doorway. Since the staircase was relatively short, it only took a few moments to hit the dirt floor below.

The shelter was what one would expect. The walls were made of white cinder blocks, and small incandescent bulbs lined the ceiling. Only a few towards the front and sporadically towards the back remained after what Hawke assumed was Killian's outburst earlier.

Hawke scanned the room and noticed the canned rations and other goods the villagers had stored in here strewn across the floor. Seconds passed, then he heard the villagers come down the stairs and drop off the other soldiers. They rested them against the wall, then quickly made their way back up, closing the door behind them.

"If this doesn't scream 90s horror film, I don't know what does," Hawke muttered as he scanned the room for any sign of Killian. He looked to the far right, and as he turned his head to scan the other side, he was greeted with a surprise.

Killian stood in front of him.

However, there was something different.

Instead of the cloth he had placed around his waist, it seemed the goo that had enveloped him before had covered it.

Where the hell? I didn't even hear him move.

Hawke was able to keep his composure as their eyes locked. His crimson pupils radiated with hunger and rage. It was as if he were face-to-face with death itself.

"Killian," Hawke stated slowly.

Killian moved his face closer until Hawke could feel the man's breath on his cheek.

"Leave."

His voice was strained and barely audible through his clenched teeth.

Hawke sighed.

Even though the hunger he felt was driving him mad, Killian was still able to hold his sanity long enough to warn him. That just made Hawke's decision even easier.

Killian started to back away, but as he turned, Hawke grabbed his shoulder and leaned in to whisper in his ear. "I don't run."

Before Killian could truly register what he said, Hawke threw the body from his shoulder to the floor. The shock of hitting the ground made the soldier groan and come to his senses. His eyes opened slowly but shot open when he looked up.

It was as if Death and Famine themselves stood over him with their crimson and Egyptian blue eyes.

Killian looked back at Hawke. "Why?" He asked, again through clenched teeth as his hunger continued to grow.

Hawke placed his hand on his hip and smirked as he said, "This world is built on the strong eating the weak." He looked down at the soldier, then back to Killian. "This is no different."

Killian's eyes grew wide as he looked back down.

He wanted to feed.

So bad, in fact, that his mouth started to water at the thought of devouring the succulent flesh before him.

"Please," the soldier pleaded as he reached towards Killian.

POP!

"AAAHHHH!" The soldier screamed as he kicked and rolled to his side.

Killian wasn't sure what happened until he looked back and saw Hawke with his handgun, which had a small silencer attached.

The sweet and luscious aroma of blood filled the shelter within seconds. Killian's fangs dripped as his breathing quickened. His hands tensed, subtle claws extended from his fingers. Even the goo that had covered him grew from his waist down his legs, covering him like a pair of pants.

That was all it took.

His sanity was broken.

He dove forward, his fangs bared, but they quickly vanished beneath the flesh of the screaming soldier. Blood rushed down Killian's throat, making his lust for more intensify. His lust grew so deep that he didn't even hear the screams or notice the ooze extend past his lower body and almost envelop his victim. However, the man's cries slowly faded into nothing more than a whimper as the last bit of life left his body.

Meanwhile, Hawke didn't move.

In fact, his eyes remained focused. Even though he had been through a lot in his life, nothing could explain why death, even as it happened right there, never bothered him.

In an odd way, he found it invigorating now.

Killian released the man's neck, allowing his body to make a thud against the ground.

One wasn't enough.

He needed more.

As the body lay motionless, the abysmal fluid surrounding Killian's lower half began to melt towards the corpse. Hawke couldn't tear his eyes away as the body seemed to liquify beneath that terrifying muck. He could see the flesh melt from the bones before they even vanished into nothing. The ooze then slowly moved back to its host and covered him tightly from the waist down.

Hawke kept his composure.

He would deal with the Venom-like fluid attached to Killian once he was sure he wouldn't go feral on him.

The other soldiers behind him started to wake up. They shook their heads to regain their senses but panic quickly set in when they made eye contact with Killian.

His pupils dilated slightly as he darted forward. The scene resembled a panther attacking baby gazelles.

They had no chance.

Their screams mirrored the man from earlier but intensified as the flesh tore from their bones.

The screams echoed through the walls, but the mixture of breaking bones and tearing flesh almost made a horrific symphony of chaos.

Within moments, the men's screams stopped. Killian ripped and gobbled up the flesh from their bones as the ooze partook of the organs. Though it shifted, it never separated from him altogether. It seemed that it needed to remain in some form of contact with his body.

The bodies began to disintegrate just as the first one had, vanishing within a pool of depth and sorrow.

As all this unfolded, Hawke stood back and watched. He needed Killian's hunger to be manageable if his 'plan' was going to work.

Well, if one could even call his idea a plan.

It was more like a gamble.

One that could cost him his life.

Moments crept by as Killian and the parasite finished up their meal. The ooze returned to its original place as Killian proceeded to stand up straight. The way his body, bare except for the ooze and blood that covered him, radiated against the pale light from the bulbs was supernatural.

He'd truly evolved into a nightmare.

Killian's head turned quickly, meeting Hawke's stoic eyes. It was only for a second before Killian leapt towards him, claws reared back and ready for bloodshed.

Hawke dodged, feeling the wind from the swipe in front of his face. He quickly crouched and used his leg to sweep Killian's right foot from under him. Killian regained his composure instantly as he jumped back, using his right hand to push his body from the ground. Hawke, not giving him a moment to compose himself, leapt forward and reared back his right hand into a fist. He lunged with his bodyweight behind his strike, but Killian dodged to the left.

Killian, now on all fours, crouched on the ground, then leapt to the right and to the left, quickly lunging towards Hawke with both hands reared back. Hawke dodged, but not fully. His shirt tore as the dagger-like claws caught the fabric and a bit of skin. A wince was all he gave as a small stream of blood slowly trickled down his chest from the three slashes.

Smelling the blood, Killian turned back and lunged again. Hawke couldn't regain his standing fast enough to dodge. Instead, he grabbed Killian by the wrists as he fell to the floor. Killian leaned in close, snapping his fangs at Hawke's face, trying with all his might to get a piece of him.

It took everything Hawke had to keep him at bay.

He had to act, and he had to act now!

"Killian!" Hawke yelled as he struggled. "Killian, you have to listen to me!"

Killian ignored him as he continued to snap at him.

"You are stronger than this! The Killian I know wouldn't let some 'science experiment' get the better of him. He would turn this downfall into a strength and find a way to use it to his own advantage. That's what Killian Blackwell would do!"

As he spoke, Killian could only make out a few words between his internal lust for more.

Kill. Kill. Kill.

His thoughts were jumbled, but he was able to focus long enough to hear his full name leave Hawke's lips.

My....name

He paused, almost going limp against Hawke's arms.

Hawke was taken aback by the sudden change but used it to his advantage. He threw Killian to the right and quickly jumped back to his feet.

Killian, however, did not get back up.

He sat on the floor with his fists tightened, his arms and legs resting beneath him. His teeth were clenched tightly as his growls began to slow and his breathing became ragged.

"I...will....not...", he softly whispered through his clenched teeth.

"BE USED LIKE THIS!" He yelled towards the ceiling at the top of his lungs as he leaned back. Blood gathered and seeped from his eyes. The tears strewed down his face. The bright red of his blood morphed into the darkness of the ooze as they dripped to the ground.

The ooze around his lower half moved with grace as it enveloped him fully.

And what he morphed into was horrific.

His head took the shape of a wolf's skull while his arms extended into thin, bone-like appendages. As he stood, his body stretched as his legs grew long and his knees inverted like an animal. His feet morphed into beast-like claws, which matched the protruding bone talons extending from his hands. Black sludge dripped from him just as it had with Amos as he stood and showed how disgusting and horrific he had become.

Hawke stepped back as Killian cocked his head towards him and lunged once again.

This time, however, it was different.

It wasn't as feral.

It was stronger and more calculated.

Which made it that much harder to counter.

Killian's claw came down with force as Hawke dodged, but only barely. The ground beneath them shook, and deep incisions formed in the ground beneath Killian's claw. Hawke regained his footing, and once he noticed the slash marks, he knew he needed to get through to him quickly.

Otherwise, he wouldn't make it out alive.

Killian lunged again and again and again. Each time, Hawke was able to dodge or parry his way from death, but he wasn't able to dodge completely every time. Minor cuts and lacerations formed along his arms, chest, and face.

"Killian!" Hawke yelled as he continued to dodge. "You're almost there! You can fight against whatever this is!" He turned on his heel and punched towards Killian's face, only to be blocked by his arms. The force of the hit was able to buy him enough time to expand the distance between them, though.

His breathing ragged and his clothes ripped, Hawke stood firm. His dedication and pride never wavered.

He realized talking was getting him nowhere, so he had to think of something else. Unfortunately, his second idea wasn't much better than the first.

As Killian readied himself for another attack, Hawke stood tall and did the unthinkable.

He relaxed his defensive stance and relaxed his arms at his sides.

"If you cannot win against this thing inside you, then what use do I have for you as a rival?" Hawke's tone was cold and emotionless.

Killian leapt towards him, his claws drawn back. He did nothing but keep eye contact, and as Killian's hand came down...

Nothing happened.

He stopped his attack inches from Hawke's face. His breathing had calmed, and the bloodlust was gone.

He had come back.

Neither of them said a word as his body started to melt away.

Piece by piece, the ooze and bones fell to the ground. Soon, Killian stood in his human form.

The ooze seeped into the ground and linked itself back to his body. This time, it covered more, leaving only his head and neck untouched.

After a second or so, Killian was the first to speak as he stood up straight and, with a rather unamused grin, said, "You are so fucking dumb, you know that?"

Hawke snickered as he crossed his arms, and a smug look came through. "And you're so fucking weak that you let something like a virus overtake you. Talk about pathetic."

Killian snickered. "I guess this round goes to you." He paused after he turned around, his back now to Hawke. "How did you know I wouldn't kill you?"

Hawke moved forward and placed his hand on his shoulder. "'Cause I knew you were in there. You just needed to regain control while you were in berserk mode. If you could, I figured it would be the final nail in the coffin for whatever animalistic tendencies were infused into the virus."

Killian was honestly baffled. "You thought of all that?"

"Yeah," Hawke nodded before he put both hands behind his head and started towards the entrance. "Saw it in an anime once. Figured it couldn't hurt to try. Everything else that's happened to us has been crazy, so why not?"

Killian let out a laugh as he too walked towards the entrance. "Why am I not surprised it was something as simplistic as that?"

They continued with a few more remarks as they opened the doors to the shelter and emerged as the calm blanket of dawn enveloped them. The small rays of light allowed Hawke to really take in how Killian looked. The intricate patterns and details throughout were so impressive that he couldn't help but whistle.

"I gotta say, dude, I am kinda jellin' over how badass the new bodysuit looks. Not so much for the asshole inside, but ya know," he stopped and smiled as Killian too examined his new body.

He stared at his hands, then up his arm to take in the definition of his physique outlined in great detail. He was genuinely baffled by what covered him.

He would've kept examining his new body had he not heard a slight rustle of footsteps.

Hawke and he both looked forward and saw the village elder walking towards them. It wasn't just him, though. The whole village had come rushing out when they heard the doors open.

The elder stopped a few feet from them both. "Mr. Blackwell?" His voice was shaky with the emotion behind his subtle question.

Killian locked eyes with Hawke for a moment before he smiled and walked towards the older man. He crouched down on one knee and placed his hand on his shoulder. "I'm back, old friend."

Tears flowed down the elder's cheeks as he smiled brightly. The other villagers soon joined in as they ran towards him with smiles and tears galore.

15

The Plan

A few hours later...

Hawke rustled through his belongings in what was left of the house they'd been staying in. The back wall and half of the roof had been destroyed, but most of it still stood. Had to give the villagers credit. They knew how to build sturdy houses.

Though he was merely there to grab a few things while Killian talked to the elder, he couldn't help but wonder why it was taking so long. The feeling he had in his gut was never wrong, and it was gnawing at him with full force.

He paused and looked over to the door.

"He's probably just taking a little longer since all the villagers were anxious to see him," he muttered under his breath as he pulled a handgun from his bag. He cocked it back and looked down the barrel before he placed it in the holster on his side. With a deep, aggravated sigh, he slammed his hands on the table.

"Damnit," he said as he then left the living room and darted out and slammed the front door behind him.

Once outside, he noticed most of the villagers were cleaning up the leftover debris. Most were moving the stray wood and metal from the destroyed houses, while a few of the men moved the enemy's bodies in a pile near the center.

His eyes wandered until he noticed the line of bodies covered in small sheets lined up to his left. They stayed focused for a moment before he mumbled, "Sorry for not being able to save you."

"Hawke?" A soft, familiar voice chimed in behind him.

It was Clarice.

Without thinking, Hawke quickly embraced her.

Clarice did nothing right away but smiled and returned the hug gently.

Hawke realized what he'd done and retreated a few steps. He coughed into his hand as he averted his eyes. "I'm sorry," he said.

She laughed slightly. "It's alright. I understand you were worried about us." She looked behind her at the commotion going on. "A lot happened last night," she said before she looked back, "and it's partially thanks to you that we can look forward to living another day. Thank you." The emotion behind her thanks was evident. It sounded like she was on the verge of breaking down.

Hawke noticed and could tell that her thank you was truly heartfelt. He also knew she was only keeping it together for the sake of the other children.

She was a strong woman.

He smiled softly. "You don't have to thank me," he said.

As he was about to continue the conversation, he caught a glimpse of the elder off in the distance. "I'm sorry, but I have to go," and with a nod, he darted past her.

"Be careful, Hawke," she yelled as she waved.

"I will," he responded with a wave of his hand.

It only took him a few seconds to catch up to the elder.

"Sir!" he stated as he stopped behind him.

The elder turned and smiled. "Why hello, Sir Hawke. What can I do for you?"

Hawke looked around but didn't see Killian. "I thought Killian was with you."

The elder looked somewhat confused before he used his cane and pointed towards the forest. "Mr. Blackwell left my company quite a while ago. He said he was going to the lake to scout the area."

Hawke clenched his fists before he let out an agitated sigh. "Thank you!" He yelled as he ran in that direction.

"Damnit, Killian," he said between his breaths. "Why did you go out alone?" His mind began to race with possibilities.

He could be dead from a rogue soldier.

He could be man-snatched again.

He could even be...

He stopped the last thought.

"You can't fuckin' die now, you prick!"

His mind continued to think of all the outlandish things that could've happened as he broke through the treeline at the lake. He lifted his hand as his eyes took a moment to adjust to the bright sunlight, but when they did, he stood stoic at the sight he beheld.

There, standing at the end of the dock that Hawke knew all too well, was Killian.

It seemed as though the armor that clad his body still had its hold on him. The sunlight glistened off the almost metallic hue as the rays highlighted his silver hair. The air around him nearly seemed sentient.

What really made the difference, though, was the expression he wore.

It was that of a warrior who had seen countless battles.

And that of one who was fighting an unimaginable battle inside himself.

"I know you're there, Hawke," Killian stated. He didn't look back, though. His eyes never faltered in their forward gaze.

Hawke sighed and casually walked to stand beside him. "You could at least tell the person who was waiting on you where you went, ya know?" Though he spoke, he didn't make eye contact. He stopped beside him and joined his gaze.

"I know," Killian remarked with pain behind his words. "I just needed to think." He paused as he looked down at his hands.

"It took me years to become the man I was before this mission. To be the man I needed to be to take my position in The Syndicate. To instill fear in everyone who heard my name." He clenched his fists tightly.

"Now I've been turned into this *thing* and can't even control my own emotions, let alone anything else. It's like starting back from square one." He snickered slightly as he looked over to Hawke. "I'm even having a heart-to-heart with a CIA Operative. What else could happen, right?"

Hawke said nothing as he met his gaze.

Killian was right, though.

Over the last month, they were kidnapped, experimented on, and attacked, and that was just the tip of the iceberg.

Hawke looked back across the lake. "I can tell you've changed. In fact, I think maybe I don't hate you *as much* as I used to, and that's conflicting for me. Before, I would've had no hesitation in killing you if the order was given, but now…" He turned his body to face him.

"It looks like you're gonna have to rebuild yourself from the ground up and find a way to deal with what you are now. But just know," he paused as he placed his hand on Killian's shoulder, "while we're here, I have your back. I want to get home as much as you do." He smirked as he met Killian's somewhat puzzled gaze. "We might as well be brothers-in-arms at this point."

Killian's confusion was understandable, but then again, he made a point.

They'd been through so much that no one would understand.

No one else could even begin to fathom the level of bullshit they'd been through. But for some reason, knowing he had someone like Hawke having his back while they went through all this was rather comforting.

"Guess I can't argue with that," he paused as he turned and extended his left hand. "Brother."

Hawke snickered and took his hand from Killian's shoulder, and firmly grasped their hands together. "Of course, you can't argue with that. I do have my moments after all."

"Though they may be few and far between," Killian retorted.

"Only from your point of view," Hawke responded.

Killian snickered under his breath and looked back to the lake. For the first time in a long time, even before this whole cluster fuck of a situation happened, he felt...content.

But only for a second.

A sharp pain stabbed his back as he fell to his knee, his hand still within Hawke's grasp.

"Killian!"

His breathing was ragged and sporadic as he clenched his jaw.

"What...the...hell..." was all he could muster between the shocks of pain as they coursed through his body.

It took Hawke a second, but he noticed the black ooze around Killian started to move. The intricate designs began to recede and bubble. He watched as it crawled up his arms, over his shoulders, and gathered into a mass atop his back.

Without thinking, he released Killian's hand. This caused him to fall to his hands and knees as he tried to restrain the screams he wanted so badly to release.

Hawke couldn't take his eyes off him. The way the ooze moved was almost hypnotic. It continued until it outlined Killian's spine in a beautifully scary design from the base of his neck to his tailbone. It nearly mirrored the shape of his backbone but pointed on the edges. It flattened down and sat almost flush with his skin. One could even mistake it for a tattoo if they caught just a glimpse.

Once it stopped moving, Killian was able to breathe. He gasped for air as the tension in his muscles released, and he almost collapsed to the dock from exhaustion.

Hawke backed up a few steps and stared down at him. "Every time I think I'm used to this, you just pop up with something else that makes me wonder if it's a good idea to leave you alive."

Although he said his statement in a relaxed tone, Killian knew he was only partially kidding.

He snickered as he stood up slowly and pushed his bangs back from his face. "I know, and honestly, that is one of the biggest reasons I respect you now." He paused as he walked closer and stopped face-to-face with him.

"I know that if I ever turned into the monster they wanted me to be, you wouldn't hesitate to put me out of my misery. And for that, I'm grateful."

Hawke smirked before his eyes couldn't help but look down. It hadn't clicked in his mind yet that, since the ooze had receded, nothing was covering the front.

He took a long stride back as he looked to the far left and sighed. "Well, now that that's over, could ya please put on some clothes. This whole 'you being butt-ass naked' thing has got to stop."

Killian couldn't help but laugh out loud at his remark.

He didn't say anything, though.

In fact, while he still wore a smile, he walked over to the small stack of clothes he had brought with him and put them on one by one. He had come to the dock not just to take a minute for himself but also to see if he could figure out a way to control his new permanent assistant.

Apparently, when he felt safe and his body was relaxed, the ooze retracted.

Good to know for later at least.

After a few moments, he turned back to Hawke, fully clothed. He outstretched his arms to his side and snickered as he said, "Better?"

Hawke, who had turned around by that point, turned back and sighed. "Much. I can only take the rated R version of you so many times, man. Ya gotta work on that."

Killian laughed as he walked over and placed his arm over Hawke's shoulder. "You know you like seeing me naked. You don't have to lie. It's just us guys out here."

Hawke sarcastically snickered as he darted out from under his arm. "You just keep telling yourself that. I'll stick to my current side of the field, thanks."

With a shrug and smile, Killian walked past him and started towards the village. Hawke quickly picked up his pace and darted past.

"Now let's go back to the village and devise a plan on how to show that doctor why you don't fuck with us," Hawke said with a rather amused look on his face.

"I like the sound of that," Killian stated as he crossed his arms. "Let's show them all why you don't fuck with a Blackwell," he smiled maliciously, then glanced over to Hawke as he continued, "or an Everhart."

16

The Night Before

Back at the village...

Killian and Hawke made their way through the trees and emerged near the center of the village.

Which was turning out to be a usual occurrence for them.

In the little bit they'd been gone, it seemed the villagers had made quite a bit of progress. Smoke towered from a large fire that burned near the center. As they approached it, a distinct smell filled the air.

A smell they both recognized and equally despised.

The smell of burning flesh.

Killian stopped one of the men walking by and asked to verify. His hunch had been right. The villagers had decided to burn soldiers' bodies along with all the broken wood and unusable items from the attack.

Hawke walked a few steps closer and stared into the base of the flames. He could still make out a few of them.

Killian popped up beside him and also allowed himself to be lost in its beauty.

They stood in silence before Hawke asked, "Are the villagers in there, too?"

"No," Killian answered. "Their bodies are sitting near the river now. They will be buried in the cemetery."

"Good," Hawke responded as the flames danced against his eyes. It took him back to a moment in his own life that he tried time and time again to purge from his memories. He sighed as he shook his head slightly and looked away. "So what do we do now?" He asked while he watched one of the young boys run towards his mother's arms.

Killian's gaze didn't falter as he said, "We destroy them."

The rather matter-of-fact way he said it made Hawke turn back around. The expression plastered on his face was one Hawke had seen many times through his photos.

It was the look of a cold-blooded murderer.

As Hawke was about to say something, the village elder popped up behind them.

"Excuse me, Mr. Blackwell."

Killian looked back and smiled with his regular expression. The fact that he changed it so quickly was rather amazing to Hawke.

Kinda scary too if he was being honest.

"Yes, elder," Killian responded as they both turned to face him.

"The other villagers and I were wondering what your next move is going to be." As he spoke, the men from the village slowly gathered behind him. The look in their eyes was one of sorrow, mixed with hatred and a hunger for revenge.

A look that both of them had worn before.

Killian paused but then stepped forward to address them.

"You have served me and The Syndicate with unwavering loyalty for as long as I can remember."

His voice was bold and powerful.

Everyone stopped what they were doing, and all attention was his.

As he spoke, he walked and appeared to acknowledge every man who stood there.

"I have seen some of you grow into the men you are today. I have seen you have children of your own, and on more than one occasion, I have seen you defend this village with your lives. This time is no different," he declared as he stopped on the other side of the group and turned to face them.

"The enemy has attacked and taken your family and friends away from you. They have destroyed your homes and insulted the hard work of those who came before you. They have insulted The Syndicate. They have insulted me." His own anger and desire showed through as his eyes started to glow ever so slightly.

"I will not allow those who have dared spit on my name and the work of this village to go unpunished. You are part of The Syndicate. You are MY people, and I won't allow anyone to desecrate anything that is mine."

Hawke did nothing but watch. He could see life coming back to them. Their eyes burned with fire from his words.

"We are going to destroy them and everything they've built. Not one of them will be left alive. We will remind those who have gone against us why we are feared worldwide. We will remind them why you don't go against The Syndicate. We will remind all of them why you don't go against KILLIAN BLACKWELL!" He yelled as he raised his fist in the air.

Cheers and yells followed as every man raised their own fist in unison.

Killian smiled as he saw the life flow back into his men.

Hawke couldn't help but feel the fire from their spirits. He hated to admit it, but Killian wasn't too bad at public speaking. In fact, he truly believed that everything he'd said was true.

Killian walked back through his men, patting a few of their shoulders before he stood next to Hawke. He crossed his arms and smiled.

Hawke, as his gaze continued to look towards the group, leaned in closer and whispered. "So how exactly do you plan on destroying them, fearless leader?"

With his smile never breaking, Killian whispered back, "I think I have an idea, but I'll need your help." He looked over to Hawke. "Would you be up to causing some chaos?"

Hawke met his gaze and smiled. "As long as I get my shot at the bitch who did all this, I'm up for anything."

"Great," Killian said as he turned around and gazed back at the tower of flames. "'Cause it might just take everything we have to pull this off."

The next morning...

Hawke let out a rather long yawn as he stretched his arms out above him.

It had been a very long night.

Everyone, including the elder and a few of the villagers, had stayed up devising the best way to attack the enemy village. To make it easier for everyone involved, they had moved one of the large dinner tables to the city center and allowed anyone who wished to join in to share their opinion.

Hours had gone by as they argued, debated, and even had a couple of rock, paper, scissors decisions in the mix.

Finally, though, they had decided on a plan and worked out the details as the sunlight peeked out over the horizon.

"So do we all understand our parts in this?" Killian asked as he let out a yawn himself.

Everyone, the villagers, Hawke, and the elder, nodded.

"Good," he stated as he stretched out his arms. "We move out late tonight. Everyone, go home, get some rest, and make sure your family knows you love them." His expression turned serious.

"It might be the last time you see them."

He could tell the villagers understood as they dispersed and headed back to their homes. Hawke and Killian remained there for a few minutes, though. Hawke sat in his chair as he watched them all go to their families.

A slight sting hurt his chest at the thought of a family to go back to.

Although Killian didn't look over, he could tell Hawke had something on his mind just like him. "Let's head back and get some rest," he said as he started to walk away. "They have us set up in one of the houses with all four walls so we can actually get some sleep too."

Hawke couldn't help but break his thoughts and laugh as he stood. "Sounds like we got moved up to the penthouse suite then." He caught up to Killian and just walked beside him. "I can't wait to sleep in an actual bed."

"Doesn't take much to make you happy, does it?" Killian snickered back.

They continued their banter until they made it to the house.

Their demeanors changed once they were behind closed doors, though.

The air became thick as Killian, with his back to Hawke, removed his shirt while Hawke looked through his bag on the table.

"There's a chance we're not gonna make it out of this," Hawke said as he placed his gun beside it.

"You're right," Killian responded as he stood there with his back bare, his spinal cover softly reflecting the light from the bulb above them.

Hawke released a small sigh as he rested his hands on the table and leaned against them. "You know that I'm gonna be really pissed if we die and the last thing I see in this life is your ugly mug."

Killian smirked to himself as he reached down and grabbed a small flask from his own bag, which sat in a chair against the wall. "Then I guess that means you have to make it out of this alive, right?" He opened it slowly and took a rather long swig of the alcohol inside. He turned and extended the flask to Hawke.

Hawke smiled as he took it. "I guess so," he stated before he too took a long swig. He winced at the strength of whatever it was. He then lifted it high as he handed it back.

"Ta livin' another day so I can kick your ass."

"To living another day."

They both smiled and nodded. They knew the mission they were going on was difficult, if not damn near impossible, but they would succeed.

They had to.

17

Attack

15 Hours Later...

The villain's stronghold was silent. The only sounds were the occasional footsteps of soldiers as they made their rounds along the perimeter. Only a few were keeping watch as the others were indisposed inside the small makeshift houses. Lights from inside showed most were drinking, playing cards, or other questionable endeavors.

Along the outskirts, the sound of nature melted with the almost silent footsteps surrounding them.

The villagers lay hidden in the trees as moonlight softly accentuated their gear and weapons.

Luckily, the elder had decided to keep the uniforms and weapons from the corpses.

Said he figured they would need them.

And he was right.

The men stood at the ready as they almost had to hold themselves back from running in headfirst and attacking without mercy.

"Seems like you were right," Killian whispered as he looked through his night vision binoculars. "They only have a few soldiers surveying the area, and the way we escaped last night is unguarded."

He handed the binoculars to Hawke, who quickly surveyed himself. "I knew I'd be right. It's typical when the enemy thinks they have you backed into a corner. Their defenses soften," he whispered as he handed the goggles to one of the men, who put them away. "Let's move ahead as planned."

Killian turned towards the villagers. He made a few hand motions to signal the start of the mission, and they dispersed within seconds.

"I still can't believe we're doing this," Hawke remarked as he readied his handgun.

With a smirk, Killian did the same as he looked forward. "Especially with you as my partner."

Hawke snickered before he took a deep breath to ready himself.

"Let's go," Killian stated.

They darted through the darkness towards the building, making almost no sound at all.

Since the night watch was so small, they had no problem getting to the entrance they'd used before. They jumped through the windowless opening, and once crouched, Killian reached up and clicked his small flashlight twice.

He receded back, and they both covered their ears.

BOOM!

A loud explosion went off near one of the huts on the other side of the village.

Soldiers ran out quickly and headed towards the explosion. Gunfire filled the air as the villagers took them down one by one. However, it didn't take the soldiers long to catch on.

They armed themselves and quickly opened fire in retaliation.

As the bullets darted back and forth, Killian and Hawke opened the hatch to the underground fort and quickly made their way inside.

They quickly readied their guns as they reached the bottom.

Stealthfully, they inched down the corridor as they realized the commotion had caused everyone in the tunnels to retreat.

Which posed a problem.

Since neither one of them knew which way to go.

"So what now, fearless leader?" Hawke asked with a slight hint of sarcasm. "I don't know about you, but I have no fucking clue where anything is down here."

Killian released an irritated sigh, but he couldn't argue. The layout of the tunnels was the one thing they couldn't get their hands on before the mission.

"Let's just retrace our steps from before, politely ask for directions when we find someone." An undertone of sarcasm complemented his stoic tone.

Hawke rolled his eyes as he brought his gun to his chest and checked around a corner. A smirk broke his serious demeanor. "I think I found just what we need."

Killian, obviously confused, looked around the same corner.

There, sitting against the wall in the fetal position, was one of the scientists. In fact, it was the one who had been with Dr. White when they first met that lunatic.

A sinister smirk plastered Killian's face.

"I think you're right," Killian stated as he holstered his gun to his thigh and walked to the cowering man.

The man was so terrified that he hadn't noticed them standing there or even when they spoke. He rocked back and forth while he muttered under his breath.

He was out of it.

He didn't even notice Killian come up and squat down in front of him.

"Oh, doc," Killian said with a malicious tone.

The man froze.

He looked up as tears flowed down and mixed with the snot from his nose. His eyes grew wide and his pupils shrank as he realized who was standing in front of him. Fear rushed through him to the point he soiled himself as he sat there.

Killian smiled as he leaned a bit closer, now only inches from the man's face.
"I'm glad to see you remember me," he demonically whispered.

He then pulled back and, with an unsettling smile, asked, "How do we get to the generators and the servers?"

The man's fear made him choke on his words as he softly told them the servers were located five halls down on the left, while the generators required a few more twists and turns to get to.

Killian, who still wore his unsettling smile, placed his hand on the man's shoulder. "See? That wasn't so hard, was it?"

Hawke sighed.

"Of course, my location would be harder to get to," he mumbled under his breath as he turned. He took a few steps but stopped as he glanced back and noticed Killian was still kneeling.

Before he had a chance to talk, Killian said, "You go on ahead. I'll catch up."

The man's face darkened in terror as he looked over to Hawke.

Hawke glanced between the man and Killian before he continued down the hall. "Just don't take too long. We have a mission to finish."

"I know. It won't take long," Killian said as beads of saliva dripped from the corner of his mouth and his hand softly moved from the man's shoulder to his throat. The man continued to watch Hawke walk away until...

SNAP!

Hawke's eye twitched.

He continued with his gun drawn as the silence of the hall was broken by the ever-faint sound of flesh being ripped from the bone.

Moments later...

Killian wiped his mouth clean with the now bloodstained coat the scientist had worn. The man's face was half eaten, and the left side of his midsection was missing pieces. His blood had run out and rested in a puddle beneath his body.

The luxurious taste that lingered in his mouth was intoxicating, but he had to focus. Hawke had gone ahead and taken his left to the generator room, and now he needed to head to the server room.

He needed to make sure everything concerning this horrific place was destroyed.

Before he left, though, he looked down at the corpse and grabbed the man's name tag. He examined it and said, "Bryan Holt." His eyes moved from the tag back to the buffet he'd just enjoyed. "Guess you won't be needing this anymore. I'll take it off your hands." The saltiness in his voice was pretty thick as he waved the name tag, then headed down the hall.

It only took him moments with his increased speed to dart down the hall and head right into a large set of double doors. They were reinforced with steel, and what looked like heavy bolts held it shut. As he looked over, he saw a small touchpad and smiled.

As if he were heading into a lounge, he took out the name tag and scanned it. The light turned green, and the doors slowly unlocked and then opened. "Guess it was a good idea to watch spy movies as a kid," he muttered under his breath as he walked inside.

Once in, he couldn't help but be impressed by the size of their operation.

A multitude of computer towers lined the left wall of the surprisingly large room. Their lights and soft hum added a subtle sense of serenity to the otherwise hellish surroundings. Monitors lined the front and right with a large desk circling beneath all of them. A collection of TVs attached to the wall, linked together, showed the constant surveillance over the entire hideout.

"They definitely have someone with deep pockets funding this," Killian stated as he walked towards one of the many computers. He leaned down and, with little effort, logged in and began analyzing the readily available information. It mainly consisted of surveillance records and standard documentation, but he knew there was more to it.

He popped his wrist as a sly smile broke through as he said, "Now let's find what they're really hiding."

His fingers tapped quickly between keys as window after window popped up and merged into a constant flood of information. The taps rang out like a hacker's symphony until…

"Bingo," he muttered.

File after file flooded the screens.

He'd hit the jackpot.

Everything, from the initial experiments and variations to symptoms, failed testing, and even the methodology used for selecting their victims.

It was all there.

Without wasting a moment, he quickly started typing again. He broke through the firewall and began copying all of it to his encrypted cloud storage. Through his own initiative, the Syndicate had established its own servers via private satellites, making this part of the mission much easier.

He tapped a key, and a small loading bar appeared on the screen. He needed to get it all moved as quickly as possible before…

"Why hello, Killian," a soft but malevolent voice said behind him.

Chills ran up his spine as he recognized the voice all too well. He turned slowly.

"Hello, Doc. Nice of you to join me." The hatred and anger between his words was thick enough to be cut with a knife.

Which is precisely what he wanted to do to her.

"Oh, Killian, you can call me Elizabeth," she said as she remained at the door. "I feel like we should be on a first-name basis by now."

His hand twitched as his bloodlust escalated. His eyes started to darken as rage slowly clouded his mind. "I...will kill you," he stated between clenched teeth, his fangs begging to feel her flesh between them.

"Oh, you will?" She responded with sarcasm. "Well, if you want to kill me, you have to make it through my son first." It was then that a small boy came into view and stood beside her.

The sight of the boy instantly halted his bloodlust, and his heart sank. The absence behind his eyes and lack of emotion on his face were tell-tale signs she had done something to him.

"What have you done?"

The scars along his arms and the multiple injection sites on his neck were nauseating.

They had done all of this to a boy who couldn't have been older than 10.

They were monsters.

No.

She was worse than a monster.

"All I did was make him better," she stated as she rubbed her hand along his shoulder. "I took all the information I had gathered from you and the encounter at the village to create a more," she leaned down and kissed the top of his head, "perfect weapon."

As she did all this, a single tear ran down the poor boy's cheek.

It meant the boy knew what was going on but couldn't control it.

Just like Hawke at the lake.

"I'm going to enjoy killing you, you psychotic bitch."

Elizabeth smiled as she stood back and removed her hand from the boy. "I can't wait to see you try." Her eyes turned cold as she snapped and said, "Attack."

Meanwhile...

Hawke, after many twists and turned, had made it to the generator room and was almost finished setting up the last of the small bombs they had fashioned last night.

"I can't believe the village had the stuff to make bombs," he said under his breath, but then paused. "Actually, never mind. Yes, I can," he corrected.

He had almost finished wiring the last one when a soldier walked by and noticed the broken knob and slightly ajar door. "Who's in there?" the soldier asked as he peeked inside.

Hawke quickly hid behind one of the large pillars that held up the ceiling.

The soldier pushed the door open slowly as he drew out his gun.

A stroke of luck was in Hawke's favor, though. He had placed the charges facing away from the door so the soldier didn't see them right away.

But it wouldn't be long before he did.

Fuck. Why now?

"Is anyone here?" the soldier asked as he slowly rounded one of the generators. As he did, Hawke slowly rounded the other side and made sure to stay out of sight.

Unfortunately, the soldier noticed the bomb.

"What is…"

ACK!

The soldier gagged as Hawke came up behind and wrapped a wire around his neck. He kicked and tried to loosen the wire, but to no avail.

Hawke's strength outmatched his.

Within seconds, the soldier's body went limp.

Hawke threw it to the side but didn't stop there. He pulled out his handgun, and with two silent clicks, the man wouldn't be a problem anymore.

"Last thing I wanted to do was waste bullets," Hawke mumbled as he leaned down and quickly connected the last few wires. Once finished, he set and started the timer…

15:00

14:59

14:58

"That's my cue," he stated as he reached over and grabbed the dead soldier's badge. "You won't be needing these anymore." He also decided to take his ammo, gun, and bulletproof vest. "Can never be too careful," he thought out loud as he put it on.

"Now time to meet up with Mr. Monster and get this shit over with."

As he left the room, he made sure to shut the door behind him.

"Let's just hope he's finished his part of the plan," he said with a sigh as he headed down the hall.

Unfortunately, unbeknownst to Hawke, Killian had been a little preoccupied.

18

Plan B

CRASH!

One of the televisions flew across the room as the young boy threw it towards Killian. He had dodged but left himself open enough for an attack. The boy almost teleported next to him and delivered an upper cut to his left ribs.

"Ack!" Killian winced as his body was thrown against the wall of televisions and rested against the hard stone wall.

The room was completely demolished, with most of the computers and monitors either broken on the floor or hanging by wires on the wall.

Unfortunately, Killian's body had been the leading cause of the destruction.

Blood seeped from his mouth and head as he struggled to look up at his adversary. The blood from his head wound seeped into his eye and caused his vision to blur even more than it already was. His body rested against the debris for only a moment, though, before he fell back down and landed on one knee with a rather loud thud.

As he looked at the boy, he could tell he'd dealt damage and could even see some of the boy's muscle tissue showing beneath his ripped skin, but none of it seemed to slow him down.

The tears he'd seen earlier had stopped, too, so Killian had to assume the boy's consciousness was gone at that point.

And that only made him angrier.

Killian stood up, swaying slightly as he got his bearings.

"I... am...going...to enjoy...killing you," he gasped between breaths as he looked past the boy to Elizabeth.

She had excused herself from the fight and stood with her back against the doors. Her arms were folded, and a disgusting smile was on her face. She slowly tapped her heels against the floor as she drew closer to the boy. Once beside him, she leaned down and rested his chin in her hand.

"How heartless of you to say that to this poor, innocent boy," she mocked. "He's done nothing wrong, but you still hurt him." As she continued, she shifted her attention from the boy to Killian.

Oh, how he wanted nothing more than to leap forward and gouge her eyes out, but he knew the boy would be too fast in countering.

So he needed to wait...

"Oh, I....hurt him.." Killian stated with a grin on his face. "Last I...checked...you...were the....one who..turned...him into a...monster." The blood from his head continued to trickle down until small drips fell from his chin and tapped against the floor beneath him.

Elizabeth stopped as she stood only inches from him.

"Yes. You did," she stated as she slowly leaned forward to whisper in his ear. "If you hadn't escaped, we wouldn't have needed another test subject."

Killian's eyes widened as her words bore through his soul.

He knew she was lying.

He knew they would have continued the experiments regardless of him.

But...

There was a part of his broken soul that almost believed her.

And it hurt so much.

"You are the reason the boy and so many others had to die," she continued. "You are the reason countless soldiers and villagers are dying as we speak. It's all your..."

PLUNGE!

Her eyes widened as a small trickle of blood seeped from her lips.

"Guess this....is my...fault too," Killian softly whispered back as his hand bathed in the blood from her abdomen. He pushed once more.

"Gawk," she gargled as blood spewed from her mouth, and his hand protruded from her back.

Seeing her in danger, the boy instantly ran forward and kicked Killian back. His body landed hard against the computer table, which caused all the air to leave his lungs. He slowly slid down and gasped in pain as he hit the ground.

The boy pulled his master's arm over his shoulder as she collapsed to the floor, and blood poured from her wound.

Although the level of pain Killian felt would make most faint, he smirked as he watched her struggle and gasp as she literally bled to death. He couldn't help but feel accomplished...

That is until...

"Ha...haha..," the crazy bitch started to laugh.

"Why the fuck....are you laughing?" Killian asked between clenched teeth as each breath he took sent shocks of pain through his body. The bastard had broken most, if not all, of his ribs, and he knew he had to be bleeding internally somewhere.

He couldn't last much longer.

Elizabeth smiled like a madman as she met his eyes.

The sheer level of insanity even caused Killian to flinch.

"You think this...would kill me?" She asked as she used her free hand to reach inside her lab coat. "You're wrong."

Killian's eyes shot open, and terror ran through them.

"You're not...," Killian stated as he tried hard to stand again, but his body was so worn out he could only get to one knee.

"Oh, but...," she paused as she lifted the item above her head, "I am," she finished as she stabbed the held syringe into her own neck.

The fluid rushed from the needle into her veins.

Seconds felt like hours as she never broke eye contact with Killian.

TING!

The syringe hit the ground.

Laughter flooded from her mouth as blood seeped from her ears, nose, mouth, and eyes. Her arms and legs bubbled as they split in half. Her muscles and tissues seemed to melt from the inside into gelatinous sores. Puss poured out as they grew bigger and bigger.

It was then that Killian realized the boy had not moved.

"You need...to move!" Killian yelled the best he could towards the boy.

He didn't move, though.

He couldn't.

A small tear ran down his cheek as the tentacle-like appendages from her arm wrapped his neck and started to melt his skin as if to merge with him.

Hard as he tried, Killian couldn't budge.

He couldn't do anything but watch as the horror continued.

The flesh wrapped around his neck erupted and grew until it covered his face, then his head. Her clothes ripped into shreds as the puss-filled growths consumed the rest of his body. All the while, her laughter bled into his ears. Her face turned into a disgusting collection of growths as her mouth morphed into a serrated collection of teeth. Her eyes multiplied as her head grew larger. Though her legs had split, they came back together into a lumpy mound of flesh and grew even faster than the rest of her.

It took only minutes, but what was left in front of Killian was the stuff of nightmares.

She leaned her now misshapen head back and cackled. Her tentacle-like arms waved slightly as her now massively enlarged lower half bubbled and excreted pus from the sores.

Her size was unsettling as Killian looked up to see her face. She stood over 15 feet above him, almost being too tall for the room itself.

It wasn't until he looked under where her left arm used to be that he saw something even more disturbing.

Embedded in her side was the face of the young boy. Almost plastered inside her skin.

Killian felt bile rise from his stomach, but he kept it down.

He had to keep his wits about him.

With a slight smirk, he yelled through the pain, "Seems like an…improvement to me!"

Elizabeth stopped her laughter and looked down.

Her smile never left her twisted face.

"I'm going to enjoy eating you," she said with a hoarse and gargled voice.

As she finished speaking, a small slit formed in the front of her worm-like body. The skin peeled from itself to reveal a rather large set of serrated teeth. They opened slowly, revealing the acid and rotting flesh behind them.

"Son of a..," Killian muttered, but was cut off as he dodged the monster's attack.

Apparently, this large thing could move pretty fast.

"Great," he stated between clenched teeth as pain pounded through his body.

The monstrosity laughed as she leaned down, her once beautiful face even with his own. "I bet you'll taste delicious." Her multiple eyes blinked in unison as she licked the side of his face.

He shivered in disgust but had to buy his time. He didn't have much strength left and had to do all he could to....

"Heeelp..."

Killian's eyes shot open.

"Heell..."

It was then that he realized the sound was coming from the impression on her side. The face moved slowly as it cried for help.

"Helllp...."

The boy was still alive inside her!

"Oh?" she questioned as she looked down. "He's still alive," she said rather smugly as she moved closer to whisper. "Seems this body likes to keep its food fresh." The cracks and hunger in her voice were gut-wrenching.

Killian's breathing intensified as Elizabeth receded and looked down on him. Blood dripped from his clenched fists, but it wasn't red.

No.

It was black.

The small drops gathered on the floor before they melted back into him. His pupils dilated but didn't stop until his entire eye was solid black. His fangs grew longer as his own flesh seemed to melt away.

His body cracked and morphed until he showed his other form.

The one from the bunker.

Black ooze seeped from his fangs and claws as rage and bloodlust pulsated through every vein.

It was no longer a battle between humans.

It was a war between monsters.

A few minutes prior...

Hawke rounded the corner as he ran towards Killian's location.

"Why the hell did the rooms have to be so far apart?" he grumbled between his breaths. Luckily for him, it seemed everyone had either evacuated or headed outside, so he didn't run into any trouble down the halls.

Though it took him a few minutes, he finally arrived at the large double doors. He looked at the name tag he had taken from the soldier and smirked.

He said nothing as he scanned the badge at the small kiosk and waited for the doors to open. Unfortunately, he encountered another issue.

BEEP!

The pad flashed red, followed by the words "Unauthorized Access: Denied" on the front of the box.

Hawke's confused but irate expression was turned to sheer anger as he grasped the card in his hand.

"You can't be serious…"

SMASH!

Killian, still in his almost demonic form, flew through the now broken doors and hit hard against the wall behind him. Black ooze spewed from his muzzle as he regained his composure. He shook his head a time or so and walked back towards the door. It seemed he didn't even notice Hawke, who stood in front of the scanner. He stopped at the now large hole in the doors before he leaped towards his adversary.

Hawke couldn't help but pause for a few moments as he looked to the door back to the card, then back to the door again. He shrugged to himself, then threw the now-useless passcard over his shoulder.

He leaned over to peer inside. His eyes shot open, and the bile in his stomach rolled as he saw the disgusting form fighting against Killian.

"What the fuck is that?" Hawke questioned as he slowly crept through the broken doors. He couldn't help but watch the two monsters duke it out before his brain kicked back in and he shook his head.

With Killian being in the state he was, he had something he needed to do.

He shifted softly until he came to one of the very few computers left undamaged. As he clicked on the screen, he rummaged through his pants and found what he had been digging for.

A flash drive.

Hawke stared at the small device for a second as an earlier conversation with Killian played through his mind.

"Hawke," Killian said as he walked towards him. Once the plans for the base attack had been finalized, Hawke decided it was time for a rest and moved on.

"What's up?" Hawke asked with his arms crossed as he stopped between two of the village homes.

Killian reached into his own pocket and handed the flash drive to him.

Hawke looked somewhat puzzled.

"What's this?" he asked as he examined it.

"If something should happen to me," Killian started, but was quickly cut off by Hawke.

"It won't," he interjected with a stern stare.

Killian smirked as he corrected himself and said, "Should something happen where I'm unable to, I need you to put this into one of the computers in the server room and start the program." He then pulled out a second one from his other pocket.

Hawke looked between Killian and the drive before he clenched it in his hands and smiled. "Gotcha. You're saying that if you can't do the one job you're responsible for, then I have to come clean up your mess, right?"

Killian laughed under his breath. "Sure. We'll go with that." He placed his hand on Hawke's shoulder and nodded. "I'm counting on you."

"I got it. I got it," he responded before he pushed said hand from his shoulder and continued.

"You son of a bitch," he muttered as he turned around in time to see Killian bite into whatever the hell that monstrosity was. He then quickly turned back and attached the device to the computer. He got into the file and double-clicked the only icon inside.

There was a slight delay of a second or so as a small loading bar appeared on the screen. However, when it finished, all of the unbroken screens in the room turned black as a small grim reaper popped up and smiled.

Hawke couldn't help but snicker at how cute the little guy was.

He wouldn't have pegged Killian as the kind to make cute little things.

The little grim reaper's smile turned into a sinister grin as it turned and sliced into the black screen, showing a slew of numbers behind it. He jumped inside, and the cut sealed behind him. Almost instantly, a little bar with skulls popped onto the screen and started counting down.

180

179

178

177

Hawke's expression went from entertained to baffled to irritated.

"You're got to be fuckin' kiddin' me!" He yelled as he smacked the keyboard.

Due to his years of experience, he had been keeping track of the timer he set for the bombs, and behold, the timer on the screen was in sync with it.

"I thought we had more time," he said, his expression then turning to worry as he turned and realized Killian was in no state to make conscious decisions, such as escaping before the whole place blew.

There was a slight, almost minuscule, chance he could get through to him in time.

But he had to try.

As his thoughts raced, Killian flew across the room and landed against the computers next to Hawke. The black ooze seeped from the corners of his mouth as his eyes flickered between black and red.

Hawke saw this as an opportunity.

He grabbed the gun he carried from the holster and, without a moment's hesitation, fired at Killian.

The bullet missed and pinged against the monitors beside his head. Instantly, Killian's gaze focused on Hawke, who couldn't help but flinch as their eyes met.

"You have to get a hold of yourself," he yelled. "We have less than 30 seconds to get the hell outta here or we're dead and all this shit was for nothing!"

As Hawke spoke, Killian adjusted his body and leaned in close.

His large wolf-like skull was only inches away from Hawke.

Hawke stood his ground, but inside he wanted to run. His instincts were telling him to get as far away as possible.

Just like a small rabbit when the fox pins it.

He didn't listen though.

He knew he had to stay and try to get Killian to understand.

It was the least he could do after everything they'd been through.

Killian leaned in slowly, his warm breath caressing the nape of Hawke's neck. He opened his mouth, which allowed small trickles of ooze to escape.

Hawke closed his eyes as he expected the worst. Perhaps Killian was truly gone this time, and there was no saving him. If that was the case, the only thing he could do was give himself up.

It's not like he could win in a fight against him.

At the very least, maybe his body would give Killian enough strength to survive and kill that psychotic bitch for both of them.

His thoughts raced, and he accepted his fate until a small whisper tickled his ear.

"Hold...on."

Hawke's eyes shot open as the shivering and strained voice from Killian shocked him. He looked over, their faces almost touching, and noticed his eyes were crimson.

Killian was in control.

Before he had a chance to question any of this, though, Killian grabbed his body tightly within his large hand and swooped towards the hole in the doors.

Elizabeth, who had slowly made her way closer and reveled in the thought of eating them both, was taken aback by his quick maneuver and couldn't stop them in time. Her blood-curdling scream echoed down the halls as her body remained stuck behind the large metal doors.

They wouldn't hold her for long.

With each push, the doors slightly jarred loose.

The two of them needed to get out...and fast.

Killian ran as fast as he could down the hall, all the while trying to control his mind. It took everything he had to calm his rage long enough to grab Hawke, let alone make their way out of their shitty situation.

Hawke said nothing as he clenched his teeth. The last thing he needed was to bite his tongue while his body was carried like a rag doll. However, internally, he continued the countdown.

5

They passed the second-to-last door.

4

They darted around the corner where the assistant's remains rotted.

3

Killian lifted Hawke, who grabbed onto the ladder right below the hatch.

2

Hawke opened it while Killian stood beneath him but looked back when he heard the loud crash of the metal doors.

1

Hawke jumped through after he pushed back the hatch, followed instantly by Killian, who almost melted into his human form as his head peeked through. Instinctively, Hawke grabbed his arm and pulled him out just as...

KABOOM!

Fire erupted from the entrance, and the earth shook below them. The villagers and soldiers lost their balance or fell to the ground as parts of the tunnels collapsed around them.

What felt like an eternity passed within moments as the ground stopped and a deafening silence fell over the village.

Those who had been injured gritted their teeth, and those who fell in the tunnels from the collapse lay silent in their makeshift graves. The ones lucky enough to be alive slowly regained their composure and started tending to the injured on their respective side.

While this went on around them, Killian and Hawke brushed off debris from the cave. They tried to ground themselves, though the only thing they could hear at that moment was the high-pitched whistle left behind by the blast.

Hawke was the first to regain his hearing, but Killian quickly followed suit. Without a word spoken, they looked at one another and smiled as they pushed themselves up and examined the damage.

Given how bad it could've been, the current state of things was much better than either of them had thought possible.

Though there was one abhorrently obvious issue Hawke had to point out.

His eyes still focused forward, he snickered and said, "You really need to put some clothes on before we do anything else."

Killian looked down at his very naked body and laughed under his breath. "That would be a good idea, wouldn't it?" he asked sarcastically as he looked over and noticed a dead soldier outside the house. "Care to help me out and grab the body for me?"

Hawke sighed and shook his head but made his way through the door and grabbed the body. As he did, he couldn't help but remark on his own. "I will be so happy when I stop seeing you naked all the damn time."

"Oh, don't lie," Killian mocked as Hawke set down the body in front of him. "You think I'm hot."

Hawke made a single loud laugh and turned. "You're about as hot as an ice cube in the Arctic."

"Oooo, ouch," Killian joked as he removed the pants from the corpse and slipped them on quickly.

Once finished, he looked over to Hawke. His gaze quietly asked if they were finally done with this nightmare.

Hawke looked back with hope behind his eyes.

Then, without a word, they looked back at the collapsed tunnel.

It was over.

The mission.

This nightmare.

All of it.

They had finally done it.

...or so they thought.

RUMBLE!

The ground shook beneath them.

Hawke and Killian swayed as they looked back and saw the villagers and soldiers. Though they were slightly knocked off balance, they didn't seem to feel it as much as they did.

Which could only mean one thing.

Whatever was causing the rumble...

BOOM!

Without time to finish their thoughts, a loud explosion erupted down the road. In fact, it happened right where...

"No," Hawke muttered to himself.

As fear and disbelief stained their faces, they watched as the doctor pulled her disgusting form from the hole she created. Although alive, the damage to her body was evident. Pus erupted from her gashes as blood seeped from the wound to her head. She slithered out and stood tall within moments.

No one could do anything to stop her.

The sight of her terrified the soldiers and villagers. Some even screamed and ran towards the forest.

Unfortunately, it was all for naught.

Though injured, the monstrosity still had fight left in her.

She slithered grotesquely up the road towards the frightened men as the mouth on her abdomen salivated and her screech radiated through the forest.

The men had no chance.

She reached them within seconds. Her second mouth opened wide as two soldiers fell inside. The sounds of ripped flesh and broken bones echoed as screams slowly muffled to nothing.

As she swallowed them, Killian noticed two human faces slowly form on the side of the abdomen. Their expressions were riven with pain and humility.

He couldn't take it anymore.

Killian's hand tightened to a fist as his breathing deepened.

Hawke noticed but was surprised.

He didn't see the ooze surrounding him like he had with his previous form.

No.

Instead, it slowly and methodically covered his body and hardened.

It was the suit from before.

Hawke couldn't help but snicker as he looked back at the doctor. "Glad to see I don't have to fight two monsters at once."

Killian opened his hands quickly, which caused talon-like blades to form at his fingertips. "Find a way to take her down while I distract her," Killian stated as he leaned down and darted forward with incredible speed.

"How am I…" Hawke started, but stopped as the gush of wind from Killian's departure flowed around him. "Supposed to do that," he then muttered as he watched his partner-in-crime jump and attack the monster.

With each slash he landed, she was able to heal the one before. He couldn't keep up with her. There was no way they were going to win that way. Even when he tried to go for her human half, her speed and agility stopped him from landing the final blow.

His armor was the only thing keeping him alive. With each hit he took, his armor sealed the wound with ooze and covered it back, but it wouldn't last forever.

Hawke needed to find a way to take her down.

And fast.

He jumped through the window and ran down the road towards the newly formed crater. He had hoped that weapons or something similar would be nearby, since it was close to where the armory once stood. He looked and looked but to no avail.

"Where the fuck are all the weapons when you need them?" His eyes caught sight of a Jeep run aground to the side, and in the back was just what he needed.

"Bingo," he stated as he ran over and grabbed his new toy.

Killian fell to the ground as one of his gashes covered the ground in red. He was losing blood fast, and his hunger for more was growing with each hit. He didn't have much longer before he went berserk.

He needed to finish this and fast.

"Killian!" A voice yelled from behind.

He turned and was rather surprised to see Hawke sporting a machine gun with an ammo backpack.

"DUCK!" Hawke yelled as the barrel started to turn.

Killian dropped down as the bullets whizzed over him.

As the clatter of the bullets serenaded the battlefield, the screams of the doctor echoed amidst the clouds. They hit her so fast she had no time to heal before another hit the same spot. With each second that passed, pus and blood gushed from her body and painted the floor in a disgusting montage of innards and flesh.

Hawke continued as he slowly walked closer. It took him only moments to walk over Killian, who got up and watched the carnage from behind.

They had finally won.

She couldn't take much more.

BAM!

One of the bullets jammed in the barrel and stopped the barrage. Hawke shook the gun, holding on to the small hope it would help, but was quickly met with disappointment. As he realized the weapon no longer worked, he looked forward and saw the doctor slowly slithering her disheveled body towards him.

"Shit," he stated as he quickly dropped the gun and backpack before the doctor darted towards him with a shriek. She swiped at his body, but he was able to dodge. Barely though.

He quickly ran towards some of the remaining houses, but knew the beast was right behind him.

"Killian!" He yelled as he dodged another attack from the monster. "Some help would be greatly appreciated!" As he yelled the second part, he looked back in time to see Killian hunched over. "Shit," he mumbled as he slipped beneath a fallen beam and jumped towards a pile of rubble.

Saliva dripped from the corner of Killian's mouth. His vision started to blur as a black haze slowly crept in from the corners of his eyes.

His injuries were no longer healing, and the blood he lost could not be regained.

He needed blood.

He needed flesh.

He clenched his fists tightly to try to calm his racing heart and increased hunger.

But it was no use.

His consciousness was slowly slipping away.

He would soon lose control again and attack everyone.

He would become worse than that disgusting monstrosity.

He clenched his teeth tightly as small pools of ooze seeped from the edges of his eyes.

He wouldn't let it happen.

He wouldn't let his own body betray him.

They were going to win...

By whatever means necessary.

19

Boss Battle

Hawke dodged her attack and darted behind one of the few homes still standing. Though it helped hide him temporarily, it wouldn't last long.

She slithered by, her head darting from side to side as she tried to find him.

He peeked around the small corner as he watched her go to the other house across the road and attack it first. Luckily, he had been able to get behind some debris and lose her long enough to hide.

But this wouldn't last long.

He moved slowly to the other side of the house and looked up the hill.

His eyes widened with surprise as he saw a handful of the villagers. It seemed they had gathered around Killian when he fell to the ground.

"This can't be good," he mumbled to himself.

CRASH!

Hawke flinched as the doctor destroyed the house across the street and made her way to the next one. It wouldn't take her long to whittle down the options to where he'd have nowhere left to hide.

His eyes darted back towards Killian, and he was confused by what he saw.

One of the villagers was hugging the others as they ran off towards the forest. He then turned and saluted Killian, who had managed to stand even if just barely.

Killian returned the gesture, then they moved in closer.

From what Hawke could see, it looked like they put their foreheads together as Killian placed his hand on the back of the villager's neck. His other hand softly grabbed the other side and then…

SNAP!

With a simple twist of his wrists, he snapped the villager's neck.

The man's corpse almost fell to the ground, but was spared the indecency by Killian, who caught him the moment he died.

Rage swelled within Hawke...

That is, until he noticed how Killian handled the body.

Killian softly laid the villager on the ground in front of him. He grabbed each hand and, with a gentle gesture, placed them crossed on his chest.

"Thank you, dear friend," he whispered to himself as he closed his eyes and took a moment of silence for the deceased.

Then, as if a switch had been flipped, his fangs salivated and his eyes turned black.

His hunger took over.

He leaned down like a jackal and ripped flesh from the corpse. It was like a symphony played while he devoured his comrade.

As he feasted, tears slowly dripped down his face. Although his hunger was in control at the moment, his heart was still there, and it wept for his friend. It wept for the loss of a life for his own sake.

Hawke couldn't fathom what he had seen.

"Did the guy really just," he questioned, but was immediately cut off by a rather unwelcome guest.

CRASH!

The top half of the house he stood behind crumbled and fell around him. In some twist of fate, he had been spared by the larger chunks and was only slightly scratched and bruised by the smaller pieces.

However, those little wounds were the least of his concerns.

He shook off the dust as he coughed. He waved the air to dispel the rest of it when a low grumble snuck up behind him.

He froze.

Slowly, he mouthed the words *Please don't be behind me* and turned around.

There, directly behind him, was a rather large mouth hungry for its next meal.

A second passed before Hawke sighed and muttered, "Fuck."

Just as he finished his rather unhappy thought, the monster screeched and opened wide. Its fangs dripped with fluid mixed with the blood of the earlier soldiers, and Hawke somehow managed to dodge.

He rolled to the right, towards the forest, as the monster screeched again.

"Oh my god, do you ever shut up!" Hawke yelled in anger as his adrenaline pumped through his veins.

Somehow, he was still alive, and he needed to keep it that way.

At least until....

BAM!

Hawke turned as the loud crash took him by surprise.

The doctor lay on her side in the remains of the house he had hidden behind. She struggled to move as her lower half screeched and gargled due to its injuries.

"You think you can come into my village?"

Hawke's attention then moved to the left as a shiver ran down his spine.

Killian.

His voice was heartless and vicious.

"You think you can come into MY territory," he restates as the air around him almost electrifies with his words. "And kill MY people?"

Hawke couldn't help but get chills from the aura he emitted. Even more so than the feral beast from before.

And that was absolutely terrifying.

Killian continued, step by step, until he stood beside the doctor's human body. Blood and pus ruptured from the lower half as her eyes blinked out of sync, and her injuries tried to heal themselves.

He wouldn't allow that.

He lifted his foot slowly and

WAM!

Slammed it down into one of the deeper gashes down towards her stomach.

A horrific scream echoed through the rumble and treetops. He twisted and ground as each second passed, intensifying the pain even more.

"Please...."

He stopped.

"....mercy," the doctor pleaded with tears in her two main eyes.

Killian pulled his foot back.

The doctor sighed in relief but was quickly met with disappointment.

STOMP!

Killian smashed her hand and slowly straddled over her, never breaking his blood-chilling stare. His other foot stomped down on her right arm as he crouched down slowly, his arms resting on his knees, as his emotionless expression sent chills down the doctor's spine.

His eyes almost glowed with their blood-stained hue as hatred and disdain poured from them.

"Mercy?" He asked in a rather astonished tone. "You want me to show you mercy?"

Hawke moved softly just enough to get a better look, and just as he did, he saw Killian grab her chin and pull it close to his face. He could feel the terror as it radiated through her body, and Hawke had to agree it was for good reason.

Even his own skin crawled at the look on Killian's face.

"I will show you the same mercy you showed the villagers," Killian softly declared.

He released her chin and, with no pause, grabbed her throat and ripped out her vocal cord.

She tried to scream, but to no avail.

The only sound heard was the gargling from her throat as her wound started to heal itself.

Hawke watched as Killian threw the vocal cord to the side and raised his hand once more; this time, however, it came down with force.

The doctor's eyes went wide as she moved her head enough to look at her chest.

Killian's hand slowly rose from between her breasts with her pulsating heart between his fingers.

The arteries were still attached and tried to pump blood as his grip tightened slowly. Her face twisted in pain, but no sound left her lips for her voice had not healed yet.

Hawke couldn't tear his eyes away.

He thought it was finally gonna be over with one more squeeze, but then...

Killian relaxed his grip, and her breathing softened.

His rage almost boiled over as he watched what he thought was mercy being given.

But oh, how wrong he was.

Killian leaned down and looked her in the eyes once again.

"I will make you watch as your life slowly fades away," he said softly.

Almost cynically.

CHOMP!

Hawke's eyes shot open as Killian bit into her heart. Blood gushed from the wound, but he didn't stop there. He ripped off the piece in his mouth and swallowed it whole.

Then he did it again.

And again.

And again.

Until only one small piece remained.

The doctor, with tears streaming down her face, watched as he slowly placed the last piece in his mouth and

CHOMP!

It disappeared between his teeth.

One final breath left her lips as she arched her back and her eyes hazed over. Her body fell flat, and her head rolled to the side.

Hawke couldn't say anything as Killian stood up and walked past him. Almost as if he wasn't even there.

"Wait," Hawke stated as he grabbed Killian's wrist.

Killian stopped but said nothing. He didn't even look back.

Hawke then walked to stand in front of him. When he did, he was met with something heartbreaking.

Tears of blood softly caressed his cheeks as his eyes reflected the pain and turmoil going on inside.

Without a word, Hawke placed his hand on the back of his head and drew him closer. Their foreheads tapped softly as Hawke closed his eyes and whispered, "It's over."

Epilogue

6 Months Later

"Of all days for it to storm," Hawke complained as the windshield wipers tried their best to keep the rain at bay. Though he was driving a Jeep with four-wheel drive, the mountainous roads were giving him a run for his money this time. If it hadn't been for the fact that he knew the route like the back of his hand, he would've died.

No doubt.

Luckily, it only took him a few more minutes to arrive at his destination.

He jumped out with his raincoat on and stood before a large cave. The front of which was cemented off except for a small door to the left. Apparently, this had been used by the Nazis during the war and was off-limits.

Well, except for him obviously.

He moved to the back of the Jeep and pulled out a giant cooler and a dolly. After he loaded and locked up, he pushed his delivery towards the door. Once there, he stopped and looked through the peephole.

Though this was no ordinary peephole.

A small light rolled over his eye, and a small clack signaled that the door had opened. Without hesitation, he pushed it open and continued on his way.

The dank and suffocating smell of decay and rot permeated the cave.

"God, he needs to get some air fresheners or something in here," Hawke muttered as he tried not to breathe as much as possible.

Though the cave seemed untouched, it didn't take long before it was undeniable that this was no ordinary cave.

Another large set of doors surrounded by metal walls stopped him again.

He repeated the same motion and pushed the cooler through the door to its final destination.

Small lights were scattered along the walls, while large drop-down lamps hung from the ceiling. The size was similar to a gymnasium, but it felt even larger with the roof easing into a center that never seemed to stop rising.

Bodies lined the walls, hung from hooks and chains, while some lay twitching in cages. The atmosphere was terrifying, but Hawke had grown used to it after his many visits.

"Killian," he yelled as he walked past an operating table with what appeared to be the last body he brought over.

"Killi," he started, but was quickly cut off as Killian randomly appeared in front of him. "Oh, for the love of God, stop doing that!" He yelled as he sarcastically tapped his chest with his hand.

Killian said nothing, but the smart ass look on his face was enough for Hawke to respond with an insulting murmur under his breath.

"Took you a little longer this time," Killian stated as he walked on past towards one of the empty operating tables. It was apparent he had been held up there for a while.

His face was rough with stubble from his beard, and his silver hair had grown long enough to be put back in a loose ponytail. His eyes glowed in the soft light around them. His t-shirt and jeans were torn and blood-stained, which matched the small spot of blood on his cheek.

"Well, the weather didn't really wanna cooperate this time," Hawke argued as he followed behind. "It's not my fault you decided to run your tests or whatever the fuck you're doing in the middle of nowhere."

"Well, where else do you expect me to do it then?" Killian sarcastically asked as he turned around at the end of the table. "It's not like I can have a secret lab in my basement."

Hawke couldn't help but snicker and retort with, "Luthor did it."

The mix of anger and amusement caused Killian to sigh and rub his face slowly.

"Just help me get it on the table," Killian demanded.

Hawke shrugged, but inside, he was rather proud of himself. It wasn't often you could bring up a comic book reference and it suit the situation.

"You're just mad that I'm right," he said as he leaned down and unlatched the top of the cooler. He raised the lid and inside was definitely not beer and hot dogs.

But a human body.

And it was even alive.

The adult male had his mouth, hands, and feet taped and wore nothing but boxers. Both of them reached in and, in perfect harmony, placed the man on the table.

Killian locked in the hands above his head while Hawke locked his legs after they cut the tape apart.

"So what did this one do?" Killian asked.

Hawke wiped his brow and shut the lid as he responded. "Apparently, the guy was a serial rapist and would've gotten out on parole had your lawyers not magically found all the evidence needed to put him on death row."

The man on the table slowly twitched and groaned as his eyes fluttered open. He blinked a few times from the light above his face but then looked over and saw Killian and freaked out. He started to scream, his cries muffled by the tape, and tried to get his hands and feet free.

But there was no escape for him.

As if the man were still unconscious, Killian and Hawke walked away and made their way over to the large computer screen.

"Well, hopefully his meaningless life will help me get that much closer to a cure for this," Killian paused as he sat down in the chair in front of the computer. "Whatever the fuck this is. As well as a way to remove the fried chip in your spinal cord without making you a paraplegic." He side-eyed him slightly.

Hawke rolled his eyes but then placed his hand on his shoulder and patted once. "You'll find it. You might be an asshole, a dick, an evil human being, a.."

"Where was that going?" Killian interrupted at the continuing list of insults.

Hawke laughed but tightened his grip. "You're also a genius who will figure out how to get both of us back to being normal human beings."

Killian let out a small sigh as he brought up the files from his previous experiments. "I hope you're right."

"I really hope you're right," he reiterated as image after image flooded the large monitor with decapitated bodies and mangled remains.

Meanwhile...

The light from the fireplace flickered in the somewhat dismal office. A desk sat to the side with a man looking over what appeared to be only a fraction of the papers that littered his desk.

KNOCK!

KNOCK!

"Enter." His voice was deep and unbothered.

The door opened as a very well-dressed young man walked in. His walk and posture were refined, and his demeanor subdued. The clack of his shoes echoed through the office until he stopped on the other side of the desk.

"Any update?" the older man asked, though he never looked over.

"Sir. I was unable to get any information from the lab. It seems whoever attacked it also uploaded a virus which destroyed all the information Dr. White had collected." The assistant pulled a small tablet from under his arm and held it out. "We were able to get a small part of the security footage, though."

The older man paused and set the documents down. He took the tablet and examined the footage looping on the screen. A smile broke on his lips as he placed it on his desk, facing up.

"It seems we have some pests that need to be exterminated." He looked from the corner of his eye to the younger man. "Send word to our undercover agent that it's time to execute the next stage of our plan."

The younger man bowed and left the room.

The tablet rested with the video paused as the man got up and walked to a large window, which showed the starry sky and a full moon.

"It seems I didn't tie up all my loose ends after all", he muttered to himself as he placed his hands behind his back.

And as he did, the image on the screen remained still, like a photograph. The black and white detail was rather choppy, but good enough. It showed two men entering the lab together; and those two men were Killian and Hawke.

Afterword

I just want to say thank you to everyone who's gotten this far. The journey from an idea written on a scrap sheet of paper to this moment when others get to read my story has been one hell of a ride.

And I've enjoyed every minute of it.

I hope you all will join me for the next installment in the Killer≠Hero Series:

Book 2

Death Internal